THE SIAMESE MUMMY

THE SIAMESE MUMMY

KARA BARTLEY

Copyright © 2012 by Kara Bartley.

Library of Congress Control Number: 2012922495
ISBN: Hardcover   978-1-4797-5571-4
              Softcover   978-1-4797-5570-7
              Ebook   978-1-4797-5572-1

All rights reserved. No part of this book may be reproduced or transmitted in any form or by any means, electronic or mechanical, including photocopying, recording, or by any information storage and retrieval system, without permission in writing from the copyright owner.

This is a work of fiction. Names, characters, places and incidents either are the product of the author's imagination or are used fictitiously, and any resemblance to any actual persons, living or dead, events, or locales is entirely coincidental.

This book was printed in the United States of America.

To order additional copies of this book, contact:
Xlibris Corporation
1-888-795-4274
www.Xlibris.com
Orders@Xlibris.com
123410

CONTENTS

Home, For a Little While 15
Family 18
In Good Spirits 24
Biscuit's Visit 31
It's Reining Cats and Dogs 36
Another Puzzle Piece 41
The Museum 43
Grandma Abby 49
The Cat's Meow 54
Another Day 57
Out There 64
King of the Cats 66
Dream, Nightmare, or Something Else 71
Ever So Watchful 74
Return to the Mummy 77
Spellbound 82
Dr. Osiris 87
Not Safe 95
Close Encounters 96
Mysterious Disappearance 101
Before You Lose 106
Sandtrap 109
What Lies Beneath 111
The Star of Omandai 116
Time is Escaping 117
Mind Trap 126

*This book is dedicated to Elsie Stephen, who had the heart of an angel.
I'm so grateful to have known you for as long as I did.
I can still see your cheeky grandmother smile,
It is lovely*

SIAMESE MAGIC

The Siamese cat is one of beauty, strength and intellect. Their decorative points, shadows of colour and sapphire stare undeniably captivate us. With an innately cryptic allure, we are unknowingly drawn to their enigmatic presence. Their grace and majesty is unparalleled.

Their intelligence is unsurpassable. Revered like royalty, they are gods imprisoned in this mortal realm.

~Kara Bartley

PROLOGUE

Jenna Matthews stood facing the audience, while directing their attention to the large screen behind her. "You can see from the image, that carnivore damage was substantial. Almost every bone at the site was riddled with tooth impressions. Gnawing and crushing was also visible on most of the specimens. Percent representation of skeletal elements indicates that there was a minimum of six individuals present at the site: four calves and two sub-adults. Paleopathological examination at the microscopic level, using our newly funded equipment," she beamed, "confirms that there were no diseases present on any of the bones.

"After examining all of the fossils, we learned that only two individuals—one calf and one sub-adult—had injuries on the limbs; breaks that occurred prior to fossilization. There was a break just below the epiphysis in one femur of the calf, and a break in one tibial shaft of the sub-adult. We do not believe that these injuries were the result of predation, but they certainly would have weakened the animal's ability to evade a predator, inevitably resulting in their capture."

She paused for a moment to inhale the stale auditorium air.

"It is suggested here that this was a preferred kill site for the fossil cat *Nimravides* as a skeleton was later found less than twenty feet from the site, completely crushed as a result of trampling. Whether that individual was responsible for the deaths of the calves and sub-adults, is indeterminate. *Nimravides* however was the main carnivore from that area and time. Others have been found associated with death assemblages not far from our site."

Jenna looked around the room. "This concludes my presentation. If there are any questions, I'd be happy to answer them at this time. Thank you."

A large smile spread across her face as the hands lifted into the air.

* * *

With her back now resting against the cushioned seat of the airplane, Jenna finally began to relax. Her thoughts were no longer confined by the tweeds and ties of the conference hall. Visions of bones and fossils disappeared out of view as she melted into her seat. "Ahh . . . that's much better."

She turned to look through the window as the plane flew over Niagara Falls. The water ignited with colour as the illumination tower shone its lights through the darkness. It had been a long time since Jenna saw the Falls. She thought back to her childhood, having grown up in Niagara all those youthful years ago. She often wondered what had happened to her old friends, what became of them.

"Excuse me, Miss," the flight attendant said. "Would you like a drink? Dinner will be served in about twenty minutes."

"Yes, I'll have a glass of wine. Red—if you have it."

The flight attendant poured the beverage and handed it to her.

"Thank you," Jenna said, as the woman pushed the cart ahead to the next person.

Jenna's mind was officially in shutdown mode. She had just given her last presentation for the month and was extremely happy about that. Her last two days were spent in Toronto, at a conference for the Society of Vertebrate Paleontology. The presentation she gave was now over and she was flying back to Kansas where her home and work awaited her.

Years earlier, Jenna had received a Ph.D. in Vertebrate Paleontology from the University of Kansas. Her field of expertise was fossilized cats; a dream she had now fulfilled. It was a phase that started when she was quite young and one which she never outgrew. She felt a strong connection to cats as if it were her destiny to study them.

After graduating, she accepted a teaching position at the Wichita State University. Jenna spent the last six years in the university's geology department developing her own unusual brand of teaching. She was a proud hybrid of arts and science, and so whenever she could, she would incorporate creativity into her classes. Sometimes she would have the students paint their research. Other times she would have them write poems about their data. "Think sideways," she would say to them. Her unorthodox methods seemed to work as the feedback she generally received was positive.

Jenna was also a stickler for detail and good old hard work. Her classroom ethics made it difficult for some students to keep up, but she understood. She remembered the days of being a grad student, too. She was there to teach and through her students, she learned.

When she wasn't working on campus, she was either researching new material or excavating a site. Most of her digs were conducted around Kansas and Nebraska. Digging was her favourite thing to do; she felt that her hands were best kept busy when they were in the ground.

Her research brought her great notoriety, especially the fossils she found in a volcanic ash deposit just south of Lincoln.

It was a tormented scene—two fossil sabre-tooth cats in the midst of battle. Jenna imagined it: their jaws breaking the air as each one tore at the other's hide. It was a fight for dominance, which neither of them claimed. The individuals were found less than two feet apart from one another. One of the cat's fangs had been broken. The other's leg had been fractured.

Jenna remembered the scene being quite eerie—it was as if the animals had called a truce while tending to their wounds. She only wished that she'd been there to see it, to know what really happened.

What she did know, was that both animals died under a blanket of volcanic ash. A mountain on the west coast had erupted, blowing hordes of ash eastward, covering the area. The two cats never stood a chance, it was their doom.

Nine million years later—Jenna found the site and released the animals' souls from their imprisonment.

She hoped that her research would be taken seriously, but she knew that eventually the questions would come. Her youthful appearance didn't help much. She was going to be thirty-five in a few weeks, but you wouldn't know it just by looking at her. Her cropped red hair was pulled back in a tight little ponytail, exposing her young, make-up-less, freckled face. Jenna still looked sixteen and had freckles to deal with. She stared at the reflection looking back at her in the window. *Darn freckles—they've done me in!*

Taking a sip of wine, she closed her eyes. *I can't wait to get home. Tomorrow's another day,* she thought. *Tomorrow, I'll start again.*

HOME, FOR A LITTLE WHILE

Standing by the front door, Jenna set down her luggage and briefcase. She picked up the mail from the hallway table and kicked off her shoes.

"Samson, Delilah—where are you? Mommy's home!"

Two black cats appeared at the top of the stairs. With a jaunty bounce, they hopped down the steps to greet her.

"Hello my babies, did you miss me?" she said, picking them up, hugging each one.

They jumped out of her arms when a loud knock hammered on the door. Jenna peered out the window next to it and saw her neighbour standing on the other side.

"Jason," she said, opening the door. "Thanks so much for taking care of the cats while I was gone. I really appreciate it."

"No problem, Jenna," he said. "I saw your car pull in. I thought I'd come over and see how your trip went."

"It went well. You know us scientists—we're a wild bunch. Actually, it went *really* well because this time they had good wine!"

"Well, I'm glad that it went well. It's good to have you back, though."

"Yeah, home sweet home," Jenna smiled.

"So, there's a game tomorrow. Are you in?"

She shook her head. "Ah . . . I don't know."

"Come on . . . I'll let you beat me again," he goaded her.

Jenna laughed, "I don't need your help to beat you. That, I can do just fine on my own. Maybe I'll go—we'll see. I need to unpack and unwind. Hopefully by tomorrow I'll be ready to beat you . . . again!"

"Like you could," he grinned. "Hey, have you gone through your mail yet? There's something from your folks there."

"Yeah, I saw that, but I haven't read it yet."

He turned his wrist and gasped. "Oh, look at the time. I've got to run. See you tomorrow, then?" he said, running backwards down the driveway.

"See you tomorrow, rookie!" she yelled.

Closing the door, Jenna wrangled up the mail and headed for the kitchen. "Come and eat, you two."

Both cats ran past her legs when they heard the sound of kibble piling into the ceramic bowls on the floor.

"It's good to be home." She opened a can of pop from the fridge and grabbed a few lemon cookies from a box on the counter. She then picked up the mail, turned off the lights and went upstairs. *A nice, hot bubble bath is just what I need.*

When she reached the bedroom door, a sigh of relief overtook her. The night was a comforting reminder that her tired feet would soon be resting. She threw the mail on the bed and then slowly made her way to the ivory bathtub that awaited her.

Half-an-hour later, Jenna emerged from the bathroom wrapped in towels. "That's much better!" She sauntered back into the bedroom while fluffing her hair with one of the towels. Turning on the lights, she found her favourite cotton pyjamas and dressed herself. A gentle calm washed over her as the fabric touched her skin.

She unrolled the bed covers, picked up the mail and began to read. "Bills, bills, bills, junk mail, bills, ah yes—a postcard from Mom and Dad."

'*Dear Jenna,*' it read. '*We're in Spain now, enjoying the scenery as always. The weather is fabulous. Wish you were here with us, but someone has to stay and do work, ha ha. Your dad and I are very proud of you, and we wish you the best of luck in Toronto. Go get 'em, tiger! Love, Mom and Dad.*'

"Boy, they really do love Spain. How many times is this now?" Jenna's thoughts drifted back to her parents' first visit there. She remembered how excited they were. Then she stopped herself. "Forget it, Jenna. Don't think about it!"

Tossing the rest of the mail aside, she turned off the bedroom light. The moon glistened through the window, lighting the room with its gentle beams. She stood for a moment in awe of the night; it was such a bewitching time.

Her mouth set free a lazy yawn as she climbed under the covers. A deep growl emerged from beneath the sheets, startling her. Quickly, Jenna's toes scrambled towards her chest. "Ahh!" she screamed.

Samson and Delilah poked their heads out to stare at the intruding digits.

"Oh geez, you two scared me. I didn't see you there. Mommy's sorry," she said, stroking them both.

Jenna inched her body to the uninhabited side of the bed and laid down her head. Samson and Delilah reminded her of Ted and Tony—two cats she had when she was younger. They were like two plump pillows who took up most of the bed. Her comfy sleeping quarters had become their favourite siesta location.

Gazing now across the room, she stared. The moon seemed to have crept closer to the window. To Jenna, it had never looked so large. Something began to stir inside of her, feelings she wanted to dismiss. She felt disturbed and unsafe but couldn't understand why. It had been almost twenty years since she felt like that.

"Stop it, Jenna, you're fine!" she scolded herself. "Nothing's going to happen. You're going to fall asleep, and when you wake up in the morning, everything will be fine."

She pulled the covers up to her chin, curled up on one side and closed her eyes.

Although Jenna's body had drifted off to sleep, her mind was still fully awake. She thought about her presentation in Toronto and the plane ride over Niagara Falls. She could see Sampson and Delilah waiting for her, but now they were the size of panthers.

In the distance, Jason was throwing a baseball at her but she couldn't reach it. Her body was being pushed and pulled into the ground. Something was reeling her in. She was sinking into something, screaming for help, but no one could hear her. Her parents were waving at her as she disappeared into the earth, but they just stood there, smiling and waving. Then, she saw a figure pacing behind them, back and forth in an agitated manner. Her head filled with a deafening roar.

NO! she screamed. *NOT AGAIN!*

The two black cats slept silently on the bed as Jenna tossed and turned throughout the night. Her dreams were forcing her to go back in time and confront the past. But something deep in her mind was trying to stop this reversal of time.

Jenna knew what awaited her there, and she feared it.

FAMILY

The temperature was hot and the sun was blazing. It was a typical July afternoon for those living in Wichita. Jenna sat on the empty bleachers at Stamford Park with her back turned to the sun's rays. She was contemplating her future. Laid out in front of her, were all the books from the previous semester. Although classes had ended, she was preparing for the autumn term.

Brushing back her long auburn hair, she leaned over the books. Her dark brown eyes peered into the pages. Jenna spent most of the time with her nose in a book. When she wasn't reading, she was either spending time with her pets or playing baseball with the neighbourhood boys. She had recently turned sixteen and was so far, enjoying the summer.

Her family lived on a small farm in Wichita, Kansas. They moved onto the property a year ago after leaving their home in Niagara Falls, Ontario. For Jenna, it couldn't have been more different. Back in Niagara, she spent most of her days watching the waterfalls, marvelling at their beauty. Her house was only a fifteen-minute walk from the Falls, so she never had to go very far to see them. The farm in Wichita was worlds away from that. It was hot, dry and gravelly, where the only form of water came as droplets from the sky.

She also missed the hustle and bustle of tourists, although farm life was starting to grow on her. Neighbourhoods in Wichita were slightly farther apart than in Niagara, and yet the people were friendly. She knew everyone on the street.

The thing that Jenna liked the most, was the fact that her house was only a twenty-minute walk from her favourite place—The Lionhead Museum.

Jenna's mother, Barbara, was a paleontologist and had taught at the University of Toronto. A year ago, she was offered the position of Curator for the Lionhead Museum. Although it was a difficult decision to move the family, they all knew it was a job that Jenna's mother had wanted for many years. And so they packed everything up and moved to Kansas.

Jenna's mother was a beautiful woman with long, honey-blonde hair and pale blue eyes. She was a classy lady who Jenna believed would go down in history as the most fashionably-dressed paleontologist in the world. "Dr. Cosmopolitan," Jenna called her.

She was also known for her shoe collection. When questioned about her acquisition of footwear, she would simply put forth her own theory of evolution. "Just think, Jenna. If only the tallest dinosaurs were able to reach the food, and only the tallest dinosaurs were able to survive, imagine what a pair of stilettos would have done for the rest of them."

Jenna would roll her eyes and laugh. "That's . . . my mother."

A calm and relaxed woman by nature, Jenna's mother always knew what to do. This characteristic was best showcased when Jenna was ten years old, just after she fell out of her tree house.

As a result of the fall, she broke both of her arms. Fearing the inevitable visit to the hospital, Jenna hid. But her mother knew just what to do. She lured her daughter into the car with medicine-laced, pain-relieving lemon squares, feeding them to her with one hand as she steered the wheel with the other. Jenna was so distracted and subdued by the treat that she didn't realize that her mother had walked her right through the front doors of the emergency clinic.

She was a nurse, a leader, a cook and a teacher all rolled into one. Jenna adored her. The genes for disposition came from her mother. Her looks however, came from her father's side.

Jenna's father, Reid, was a tall, handsome man, with chocolate brown eyes and dark red hair.

Jenna always thought of herself as a mini female version of her father. He was a smart, hard-working, compassionate man who loved animals. His profession was a reflection of his personality. He was a small animal veterinarian who worked for many years at a clinic in Niagara Falls. When the family moved to Wichita, he decided to start up his own practice. He built a small clinic next to the house and worked from there.

Not only was he the patriarch of the family, he was also the history expert. Jenna enjoyed the time they spent together. He would tell her about Wyatt Earp, the siege of Troy and the European Crusades—all on one pot of coffee. She was always impressed that her father could make any story or subject interesting. He could take a shoelace and tell you how to knot it one hundred different ways while keeping his audience awake.

Jenna loved that her father's clinic was right next door. She felt safe with him only metres away, especially when she was home alone. Although, she wasn't really alone. Their family had adopted five pets from the veterinary clinic in Niagara Falls: Max, the Golden Retriever; Charlie, the German Shepherd; Sam, the black Labrador; and two fat red tabby cats named Ted and Tony. They had also adopted three budgies, two guinea pigs, and a bright red Siamese fighting fish. The two felines however, became hopelessly infatuated with their smaller companions. The family knew that one day the birds would disappear, and that the cats would blame their actions on the dogs. So they gave away the birds . . . and the guinea pigs . . . and the fish, just to be careful.

The fish had belonged to Jenna's older brother, Scott, who was away at university. He was a beach blonde, blued-eyed heartthrob to anyone that met him. Whereas Jenna took after her father, Scott was a distinctive male version of their mother. His charming smile and off-beat sense of humour made all the girls swoon. It was his family that kept him humble, especially Jenna, who constantly teased him about his unfortunate fashion sense.

Scott had recently completed the first year of his undergraduate program in Chicago, where he was studying environmental law. He was preparing for a 'Meeting of Minds' political debate in Springfield, Illinois and was due back home in another week. It was a perfect profession for him, Jenna thought. He loved to argue, and was extremely good at it.

Scott was a devoted big brother, he and Jenna were close. He often accompanied her to baseball games when they lived in Niagara Falls. She in turn, sat and watched his hockey games. He was always there to help his little sister, whether it was with her homework or protecting her from bullies at school. He was the perfect sibling guardian. This was Scott's first year away from home and Jenna felt lonely without him. She couldn't wait to see him and hear all his stories of university life.

Jenna and Scott's grandmother, Abigail Rose, also lived on the farm with them. She was a zesty woman with long, curving, silver locks and jade green eyes. Her wardrobe was a plethora of black unbridled clothing, with beads and jewels that accentuated her gypsy flare. Jenna admired her grandmother's style and was always amazed by her sense of whimsy.

Up until a year ago, she lived in Salem, Massachusetts in a beautiful old Victorian house. A house, that had been passed down through generations of family. Jenna remembered the house quite well as she had spent many hours visiting her grandmother there. That, and every brick of the building was painted black. It was a fascinating conversation piece for anyone who saw it. A black house in Salem—it was definitely different.

Jenna's mother grew up in the house and had many engaging stories to tell; things that had happened while living there. She married Jenna's father who was Canadian, and together they raised their family in Niagara Falls. Through the years, her ties remained strong with her mother in Salem. She wanted Jenna and Scott to spend time with their grandmother and to experience life inside the raven residence.

When the family moved to Wichita, Abigail decided that the time had come for them to be closer. She sold the house to family in Salem and moved to the farm in Kansas.

She was a free spirit however, and though her bed was there, her luggage hardly was. Abigail was an eccentric woman who loved to travel the globe, perpetually. The only thing of hers that remained in place was a small herb and spice garden that she'd planted below her bedroom window. The garden was shaped like a star and surrounded by red and white roses. It was hidden by a mass of bristly bushes that encumbered the back porch; it was best viewed from the second floor of the house.

Jenna would often look out her bedroom window to admire the flowers. On days that were windy, she could smell the fragrant mixture of herbs, spices and roses. It was a reminder that although her grandmother was away, she was still there in spirit.

Jenna's favourite part of her grandmother's travels, were her stories. On her return she would speak of animal safaris, mystical encounters and other incredible experiences—all of which filled Jenna's mind with intrigue. She was especially interested in her grandmother's tales of ancient beings and collections of rare artefacts—specifically the ancient cats. She never tired of those. With all her worldly adventures, Jenna sometimes envisioned her grandmother as a multicultural storybook with arms.

Abigail had just recently returned from a voyage overseas. Tonight, she would be making dinner for the family and telling them all about it.

Jenna's eyes now skimmed over the books. She was torn between art, history and science. She loved them all. But her mind was gravitating towards biology and physiology. Ultimately, she wanted to study cats. To Jenna, they were the most interesting creatures out there. She would have given anything to have been present during the building of the Sphinx or to have witnessed the worship of the Egyptian goddess, Bastet. She was equally intrigued by the historical events that related certain felines to pagan religions, which in turn led to her love of Halloween.

For many years, Jenna dressed up as a witch for All Hallows' Eve, and had brought along her favourite accessories: Ted and Tony. The cats had to be carried, of course, since they were not accustomed to wearing holiday apparel.

Although Jenna loved Ted and Tony, she wanted to study the Royal Points of Siam. She'd read somewhere that Siamese cats were honoured throughout Thailand and that in the beginning, only kings and royal family were allowed to own them. It was believed that Siamese cats were protective guardians for palaces and the royalty within them. *What a world,* she thought. *I wish I'd been there.*

Jenna looked down and frowned at her belly as it released several mournful growls. "I know—we'll be eating soon," she said, consoling her stomach. Jenna's mind strayed from the thought of books to the dinner table. She could see mounds of corn waiting to be eaten, surrounded by plates full of lemon squares for dessert.

Her parents were now the owners of a cornfield which stood behind the backyard of the house. Upon moving to Wichita, the family was approached by Dr. Osiris, a neighbour who lived a few roads over. He was extremely interested in the property. His plans were to manage Jenna's cornfield and two others beside it. With the help of his two sons, he would take care of all three fields. Jenna's parents didn't have any experience managing a crop, so they leased the land to him.

The family was already familiar with Dr. Osiris, as he was the previous curator of the Lionhead Museum. He retired from the position rather unexpectedly, leaving an important job opening to be filled. Jenna's mother was his replacement.

Jenna liked Dr. Osiris. He was a nice old man who enjoyed having neighbours over for corn barbeques. They were always a fun event. Everyone would meet, greet, converse and laugh. It was something her family was unaccustomed to but would attend, regardless. They were delighted to be invited.

As the year passed, Jenna began to appreciate the beauty of her family's property. She still missed her friends from Niagara but she'd made new ones at school, which helped lessen the loss. She even found time to sit and stare at the cornfield. It was peaceful and yet, strangely mysterious at the same time. She thought about how amazingly simple the organization was, and how you could still get lost inside of them.

Sitting in the backyard, was a multi-coloured swing set that had been left behind by the previous owners. It provided a connection for Jenna as it reminded her of the rainbows over Niagara.

She would sit on the swings and watch the sun escape at dusk. There was something about the sunsets in Wichita that engulfed Jenna—she found them enchanting, magical. The ribbons of colour were dramatic and seemed to embrace the entire sky. Then the spectrum would disappear and the moon would make its appearance. This transition from painted day to starry night is what impressed her the most.

Another hungry growl brought her back to the present. Jenna looked down at her watch; it was almost six o'clock. By this time tomorrow, her parents would be on a plane headed for Spain. They were leaving for a two week vacation in Madrid; one they had planned for months in advance. Jenna's grandmother would be taking care of the house until their return.

As the sun began its slow descent, Jenna knew it would soon be dinnertime. Her mind was definitely governed by her stomach, especially when it involved home cooking.

She wondered if her parents were home yet. Although her father worked next to the house, he occasionally went into town to get supplies and to visit his friend Nick at the Wichita Animal Care Laboratory. He'd gone to see Nick that afternoon and told Jenna he'd be home around five-thirty or six o'clock, about the same time her mother would be arriving home from work.

Jenna stood from her seat and stretched her body, raising her arms into the sky. She then picked up the books and placed them inside the backpack. The last one to go in was a biology manual with a portrait of a leopard on the front page. When she touched the image, her hands began to shake in an odd, uncontrollable manner. "What on Earth?" she said, dropping the book. She looked around at the surrounding area but saw nothing that would rouse her suspicions.

Picking it up, she frowned. "That was weird." Brushing off the moment, Jenna put no further effort into thinking about it. She simply packed the manual away and threw the bag over her shoulder.

As she jumped down the bleacher stairs, a weird feeling tingled up her spine. It tugged at her nerve endings, craving her attention. She couldn't quite put her finger on it but in the back of her mind, she knew that something was coming.

IN GOOD SPIRITS

After a leisurely walk home, Jenna bounded up the front porch stairs to her house.

"Hey, Jenna—you throw like a girl!" a voice hailed from the road, prompting her to turn. Her friend, Jason, was sitting on his bike gawking at her.

"Yeah, you're just sore that I keep beating you at baseball. The truth hurts, doesn't it, rookie!" she struck back.

He laughed. "Okay, fine! When are you coming out to beat me again?"

"In a couple of days. My folks are leaving for their vacation tomorrow. Things are kind of busy around here. I'll call you!"

"Sounds good, see ya!" he said, riding off.

"Bye, rookie!"

As her fingers pushed open the front door, she grinned. Waiting on the other side was Max; his mouth covered in dirt, his body wiggling from nose to tail.

"Max—have you been digging again?" she said, closing the door. She bent down and brushed the brown from his snout. "You're funny, Mister."

She then stood, dropped her backpack and poked her head inside the family room to the right of the door. Sprawled out on top of the television with his legs dangling in front of the screen, was Ted. Tony sat across the room tucked within a corner of the sofa watching Garfield cartoons beneath Ted's legs. "You guys are so cute," she gushed.

Her body suddenly straightened as tantalizing aromas from the kitchen wafted down the hallway towards her. Step by step, Jenna followed them. Her nasal passages were invaded by the smells of freshly grated cheese, homemade pasta sauce and crushed garlic. Mentally, she was beginning to drool.

She heard someone moving about in the kitchen singing some old, Italian song. Jenna appeared in the doorway and watched as her grandmother danced past the Cedar table that sat in the centre of the room. With an oven mitt in one hand and a dishtowel in the other, she twirled.

Jenna crossed her arms and leaned against the wall. She enjoyed her grandmother's youthful behaviour. "Grandma, you're such a good dancer."

She turned and curtsied, then snatched up Jenna's arms and hoisted her into the room.

"It's all in the feet, my dear. It's all in the feet. Dance, Jenna!"

Together, they shimmied across the kitchen floor.

Jenna pirouetted past the oven and stopped. "Is that lasagne I see in there?"

"Yes, and garlic bread with cheese, too. Are you hungry? You haven't eaten yet, have you?"

"No—I'm starving. I can't wait to eat! But Mom and Dad aren't home yet. I thought they'd be here by now."

Her grandmother waltzed over to the oven and looked through the window. "They called here about an hour ago. They had to do some last minute shopping for their trip tomorrow. Don't worry, they'll be here soon. Until then, why don't you go upstairs and clean up."

"Okay, let me know if you need help with anything."

Her grandmother continued to dance as she left the room.

Jenna headed back to the front door, picked up the backpack and ascended the stairs. The further she got from the kitchen, the drowsier she became. Her belly grumbled and groaned for sustenance. The stash of candies in her bedroom would have to tie her over until dinner.

Pushing open the bedroom door, she entered the room and collapsed onto the bed. A giant yawn escaped her mouth as she kicked off her shoes. She was hoping that her parents would be home soon, the lasagne downstairs was needling her taste buds.

Slowly, she stood and wandered over to the window. Placing both hands on the windowsill, she looked out into the backyard towards the cornfield. "It's so peaceful living out here."

To Jenna, it was calm, tranquil; the only exception being the storms. The biggest problem her family had thus far, were the twisters. Never in her life had Jenna experienced a tornado, but two weeks after moving to Wichita, the city was inundated with a series of funnel clouds. That on its own was a story to tell. Jenna was just happy that the property came equipped with an underground storm cellar.

Other than tornado season, there was nothing for Jenna to fear.

She gazed back at the brown plaid bag that contained her scholastic material. There were many decisions for her to make, but first she needed to eat.

In the drawer of the bedside table, was a bag full of caramel candies. Climbing over the bed, she seized a few in her fingers and took out one of the manuals from the bag. "I've got time, might as well read."

* * *

Two hours later, the front door opened. "We're home . . ." Jenna's mother yelled.

Jenna dropped the book and checked her watch. *Holy cow, it's late!* Completely immersed in her reading, she had lost track of time. She ran out of the room and raced down the stairs to greet her parents.

"Mom, Dad—finally! Where've you been? I've been chewing on candies this whole time so my stomach wouldn't pass out. Grandma made lasagne . . ."

"It smells great," her father said. "Hey, kiddo, what did you do today?"

"I went to the park, thought about school stuff. Oh, by the way, there's a message for you from Mr. Winters. It's about Calvin. He couldn't reach you at the clinic, so he called here. He said he would call back later."

"Did he tell you what was wrong?"

"No, he didn't. I guess it's not that urgent. But I'll tell you what is . . ." Jenna pointed to the kitchen, "my stomach—I'm starving. I'll set the table. Grandma's got the food ready."

They all hustled into the kitchen. "This smells delicious," Jenna's mother said. "I have an idea—why don't we eat dinner outside tonight and watch what's left of the sunset."

"I'll get the picnic blanket," Jenna smiled.

Moments later, they walked outside into the fresh twilight air. They gathered near the swing set and sat amongst the grass. Jenna spread the red gingham blanket over the ground and placed the dishes and silverware on top of it. Her family lowered the food into the centre as each one took a corner of the blanket.

Together, they ate their dinner, drank several glasses of sweet lemonade and watched the sun disappear.

"What day is Scott coming back, Friday or Saturday?" Jenna asked.

"Saturday," her mother answered. "You'll have to give him a big hug for us since we won't be here."

"I will," Jenna said. "It'll be nice to have him home." As she spoke the words, the telephone rang inside the house. "That's probably Mr. Winters calling back, Dad."

"I better get that," he said. "I'll be right back." Quickly, he stood and hurried towards the house.

Jenna's grandmother looked up at the darkening sky. "I will have to make a home-coming cake for Scottie and another for you two Spanish travellers upon your return. A ninety-eight-year-old man in Cairo gave me a great recipe. It's called Jambala cake. It's been passed down from generation to generation, to all families who have Egyptian in their blood."

Jenna questioned her grandmother's statement. "How did *you* get the recipe, then?"

With a cheeky twist in her lips, she said, "That's a secret, my dear. My secret. One day I'll tell you, but not a day too soon."

"Okay," Jenna laughed. "Well, at least I get to eat it. Hey, speaking of new things, are there any new exhibits at the museum, Mom?"

Taking a sip of lemonade, she nodded. "The museum received something a couple of days ago. It should be on display tomorrow. It's a mummified artefact but I'm unsure of the details. I haven't seen it, yet. Patrick has been taking care of everything these last few days for me. Why don't you go and check it out tomorrow."

"Jenna," her grandmother interrupted, "maybe we should go together to see this. I don't think you should go alone." Her voice was uneasy, as if she had been momentarily disturbed.

"Mom—Jenna will be fine. She knows the museum like the back of her hand, and everyone there knows her. Plus, there's security."

"That's not what I'm afraid of."

There was a long, silent pause. Jenna glanced over at her mother who shrugged her shoulders and mouthed, "I don't know . . ."

"I will go with you to the museum, Jenna. I would like to see this exhibit for myself," her grandmother declared.

"Okay," Jenna said. "We'll go tomorrow, then?"

"Yes, tomorrow."

Looking back towards the house, Jenna saw her father talking on the telephone in the kitchen. There was a look of concern on his face. He spoke into the receiver and then hung up. He stood for a moment scratching his chin. The telephone rang again and he picked it up. He spoke for another few minutes and then ended the call. Jenna watched as he walked towards the fridge and then headed back outside.

As he sat down, he lowered a plate of lemon squares onto the picnic blanket.

"Is everything okay, Reid?" Jenna's mother asked.

"That was Mr. Winters on the phone. He said that his cat, Calvin, is sick. I saw him about six weeks ago when he brought Calvin in for his annual examination. He was given his shots and was fine. It's possible that he had a reaction to them, but from what Mr. Winters described on the phone just now . . . I don't understand it."

He stood, rubbed his forehead and started pacing back and forth. "From what I was just told, Calvin got into a fight with another cat two nights ago. Mr. Winters didn't see the fight but believes that it was a much larger cat that he fought with."

"How does he know that if he didn't see the other cat?" Jenna pried.

"Well, he said that he heard something in his backyard, while he was dozing off—some sort of animal outside with a very deep growl. He said it sounded like a wild cat but he thought it was a dream. When he got up and went outside to look, he found Calvin hiding at the top of their old Oak tree. He coaxed him out of the branches and looked him over for any wounds. Apparently Calvin was unharmed. No scratches, no bites, nothing. Just an incredibly frightened cat." He looked around the yard. "Jenna, where are the dogs?"

"They're inside," she said.

"Honey, what happened to Calvin?" her mother probed.

There was a lull in his voice. "Well . . . Mr. Winters kept him inside the next night and said that everything was fine."

"Okay, so if Calvin is fine, then what's the problem? Why do you look so puzzled?"

"Because . . . he's not fine. The shots I gave him were for rabies, distemper and leukemia . . ." he said, drifting off.

"So, Calvin was well vaccinated," Jenna said.

"Yes, he was. But from what Mr. Winters just told me, it sounds like Calvin has symptoms of all three diseases."

"What? That's impossible, Reid! Calvin is six years old now and he's been vaccinated every year." With the clinic next to the house, Jenna's mother was able to help her husband when she wasn't working. She was there the day that Calvin was brought in, and so was familiar with his medical history. "Calvin is one of the healthiest cats I've ever seen. For

Pete's sake, he's healthier than Ted and Tony—and they've had every kind of vaccination imaginable."

Jenna's father looked at the ground as if he were trying to dig a hole with his eyes. "I told Mr. Winters to bring Calvin over tonight so that I could examine him. He's on his way right now."

"Can I help?" Jenna asked.

"No," he said. "We'll handle this. Why don't you go inside and see what Ted and Tony are doing. Don't worry, if we need anything—we'll let you know." He looked awkwardly happy, like he was trying to hide something.

Jenna leaned over and placed three lemon squares on a plate. "Okay." She lifted herself off of the blanket. "Do you want me to bring this stuff in?"

"No, thanks—we'll tidy up," he said. "We'll talk about this in the morning. Hopefully everything will be fine then."

As Jenna turned and headed for the house, she heard her father shout, "Make sure all of the pets are inside. Double check that."

"Okay—I will. Goodnight." Jenna knew that keeping all the animals inside was a very odd request from her father. It was a farm, sometimes the animals were out at night. Well, except for Ted and Tony who were incredibly spoiled and preferred sleeping in luxury.

She walked up the porch stairs and went into the house. With the plate of lemon squares in her hand, she searched for the family pets. Once they were all accounted for, she directed herself towards her room. It was strange, she thought, that her grandmother had been so quiet. She hadn't spoken a single word after Mr. Winters had called. And she seemed worried about a simple trip to the museum.

Jenna bit down into one of the treats as she walked into her bedroom. "Oh, these are so good." The door remained partially open behind her. She sat down on the edge of the bed and finished off what was left on the plate. The phone call from Mr. Winters bothered her, as it did her father. And she wondered who the second call was from.

Her door opened the rest of the way as Ted and Tony strolled into the room. With as little effort as possible, they jumped onto the bed and gazed at Jenna with slothful expressions. She knew that look—they were asking her to move.

"I get it. I'm in the way," she laughed. She moved the pillow aside and turned down the bed covers. Opening the drawer of the bedside table, she pulled out a book entitled, *That Darn Cat*, and then slipped under the bed sheets. Being the size they were, Ted and Tony governed the mattress. So, as not to disturb their royal sleep, Jenna moved to the edge of the bed and began to read.

* * *

Outside, the adults were still talking about Calvin's mysterious symptoms.

Jenna's grandmother stood up to leave. "I'm sure that everything will straighten out by morning. You two better not stay up too late. Remember, you have to be at the airport in the morning." She smiled at both of them. "I promise, there will be an answer soon enough." With that, she left.

The sun had disappeared, the sky was now dark. All that twinkled, were the stars.

Jenna's mother shook her head. "It's just not possible, Reid. You know this. Wait until Calvin gets here. Then you can examine him and find out what's really wrong. You know pet owners, they get emotional—frantic sometimes, over nothing. I do the same thing when our pets are sick."

He sighed. "You're right, I won't know until I see him."

"I do have one niggling question, though. Why did Mr. Winters wait so late to call you? I mean—why didn't he take Calvin to emergency if he thought he was really sick?"

Jenna's father shrugged. "He told me that the symptoms weren't there this afternoon, Calvin just looked a little off. Everything else came later, in a furious whirlwind—his words, not mine."

"That's . . . quite fast . . ." she said, doubting his words.

"I know, Barbara. I know." He leaned into his wife. "But we have another problem. I didn't want to say anything while Jenna and Abby were here, but the part that worries me even more than the symptoms, is that this isn't an isolated incident. Mrs. Wightman called right after I spoke to Mr. Winters. She said that the same thing happened to her cat, Hershey. He's sick, too. He has the same symptoms as Calvin . . . and I'm worried."

"So, that's why you wanted Jenna to get all the pets inside."

"Yes."

Just then, the headlights of a silver Buick broke through the darkness as the car entered the clinic parking lot.

"That's Mr. Winters," he said.

They stood as the vehicle came to a stop. "Reid—what are the chances that these two events are unrelated?"

With unwavering certainty, he answered. "Remote!"

BISCUIT'S VISIT

Jenna awoke to the sound of a car door closing, hurried voices, and partial darkness. She sat up and looked over at the alarm clock. It was almost three-thirty in the morning. She massaged her eyes and took a deep breath. Her body trickled out of the bed as she steadied herself and wandered over to the window.

Outside, she saw the lights of the clinic. The brightness was muffled by the blinds that were drawn. *What are they doing up so late?* She then remembered Mr. Winters and his cat, and her father's worried look last night.

Jenna couldn't sleep anymore; her eyelids wouldn't stay shut. After her body adapted to the early rise, she donned on her robe and slippers and headed down the stairs. No one was there. All the lights were out.

She clambered into the family room and turned on the lights. In her state of unrest, her eyes adjusted quickly to the glare. She found the television remote beneath some newspapers and pressed the 'on' button. Slowly, the screen came to life. Fingers poised, Jenna began to flip through the channels. Her body relaxed as she slumped back into the cushioned chair next to the sofa. First, she watched the weather channel to see what the forecast would be for that day.

"A cloudless, sunny day in Wichita," the weatherman said, "with a high of 90º Fahrenheit."

Another perfect day, she thought.

Each channel was relatively boring; most had static or coloured lines. Then she came across one of her favourite movies, *Bell, Book and Candle*. When a commercial came on, she skipped through to something else. Her fingers came to a grinding halt just as the local news station broke into a commercial. Something about the channel called for Jenna's attention. Patiently, she waited for the program to return.

Ted and Tony had followed Jenna down into the family room. They were truly, her loyal companions. Ted jumped onto the television where he proceeded to hang his legs over the screen. Tony jumped onto her lap where he began to claw at her legs.

"Tony, my dear, I am not a scratching post, and Ted—get off the TV." Looking at the two cats, she smiled. She was convinced that they were ignoring her.

She lifted Tony off of her lap and put him on the floor. She then relocated Ted to the sofa next to the chair. Just as she was about to sit back down, a heavy purr came from beneath her. Tony had stolen her seat and was now stretching his legs in preparation for sleep.

"You guys need a hobby, I think." She sat on the floor between the chair and the sofa with her arms extended out to the sides. The cats stretched out their necks as Jenna's fingers scratched beneath their black, nylon collars.

The news station came back on and the anchorman started. "This is WTZN Wichita News, reporting live. Three more Wichita residents have gone missing. Police received phone calls last night from the families and are looking into their disappearances. Missing are: Albert Balaski, age 71; Sarah Durliak age 25; and Jeffrey Murdoch, age 42.

"If anyone has seen anything or has any information, please contact the police immediately. Thirty missing person reports have been filed in the last few days. There is a growing concern for public safety. Police are warning all residents to be on the lookout for any suspicious characters or criminal activity. As of now they have no leads."

Jenna couldn't believe what she was hearing.

"In other news . . . a large, unidentifiable animal has been spotted in Wichita, possibly an escaped wild cat. Local residents are warned to keep an eye on small children and animals, and to keep them inside after dark. Local zoo officials are still looking into whether a large cat has indeed escaped. Sightings have been confirmed at eight different localities in Wichita."

The anchorman then switched to the topic of sports as he began to review the latest updates in the world of golf. Jenna turned the television off. She was stunned. "Thirty people missing in the last few days? That's crazy! How can so many people go missing without any trace?" She also wondered if Calvin's encounter the other night had anything to do with this allegedly escaped wild cat.

She was deep in thought when something outside the front of the house brushed against the window. In the family room, the window that faced the front yard, extended the entire length of the room. There were no curtains behind the glass, which meant that anyone could look in or out. Everything was clear and visible during the day. But at night, things were much different. The front porch and clinic lights were the only sources of illumination. And there were no streetlights nearby. It was very difficult to see anything at night.

Jenna looked out the window, but saw nothing.

Suddenly, Tony leapt from his seat and began to growl on the floor by the window. It was so unexpected that as Jenna jumped up in surprise, she lost her balance and fell backwards onto the sofa towards Ted. His rotund body scurried into action when he saw that he was about to be squished. He squirmed out from the cushion and hopped down to the floor where he stood alongside Tony. Together, they hissed at the window.

Jenna was bewildered by their behaviour. She'd never seen the cats react like that before. She didn't think they were capable of doing anything with their mouths except eat, groom and yawn. "What in the world are you guys growling at?" She looked closely at the window. Whatever was out there, she couldn't see it. But the cats knew it was there.

Seconds later, the bushes in front of the window started to move. It startled Jenna and made the cats' performance even more disturbing. They hissed and snarled in synchronicity. Jenna's nerves were throbbing just listening to them. She wanted to put an end to her growing anxiety, so she decided to go outside. For all she knew, it was just a mouse or a bird.

She stepped into the hallway, opened the closet and grabbed her trusty baseball bat from behind the coats. She then made her way towards the front door and opened it slowly, hoping not to disturb whatever was hiding. She was careful in closing the door behind her, as she didn't want Ted or Tony following her out. Quietly, she stepped down the porch stairs. Her bat was leading the way.

As Jenna approached the bushes, they began to thrash about madly, like something was trapped inside of them. She held the wooden weapon tightly in her hands. Her mind tried to rationalize that it was just a wayward raven or a city-sized sewer rat that was geographically challenged. The closer she got however, the more she panicked. Neither bird nor mouse could cause that much of a ruckus.

Her palms were starting to sweat. Still, she was ready to take a swing at any moment.

Then, in one hurling leap, a large dog vaulted out of the bushes towards her. Its ferocious jaws barked incessantly. She jumped back in fear of being bitten and fell onto the grass. It was Biscuit, the Great Dane from down the street. Although known for his gentle demeanor, right now he was acting abnormally aggressive.

Just as he was about to lunge at her, something by the road distracted him. Together, they both looked towards the street. Jenna saw nothing in the darkness. When she gazed back at Biscuit, his behaviour had changed. He backed away from her in a subservient manner, and then yelped as he turned and ran from the property. Jenna noticed that one of his back legs was dragging on the ground. He was whimpering, groaning, limping like an injured person.

She stood slowly and calmed herself. Her question was answered: Biscuit was in the bushes. Then, like a giant snowball gaining speed down a hill, all of the other questions descended upon her. *What just happened? Why would Biscuit attack me? Why was he here? Why was he hiding in the bushes?* She had to stop herself. Right now, she didn't have any answers. Jenna knew the dog well, but had never seen him act like that before.

She watched as Ted and Tony returned to the sofa. "Great security work in there, guys. I guess that's deserving of a nap," she laughed.

Jenna didn't notice it right away and it wasn't clear until she looked *at* the window instead of into it. A thick layer of white foam dribbled down the glass. She took a few steps closer. It was right next to where Biscuit had been.

Drooling was not an uncommon trait in dogs, but this seemed different somehow. She looked carefully at the glass and noticed markings on the windowpane. They looked like scratches—deep scratches, as if Biscuit had been clawing his way into the house. "That's weird."

Jenna pulled a tissue from her robe pocket and dabbed it in the foamy spot. She then turned and walked back towards the porch stairs. *Why did Biscuit's behaviour change so dramatically?*

She climbed the steps to open the door. With one hand on the doorknob, she stopped. Her ears perked when something behind her moved. Looking around, she saw only black. She couldn't ignore her intuition, though. It was telling her that something was out there.

Opening the door, a sigh of relief overtook her. The walls, roof, floors and doors were once again her security blanket. Nothing would ever breach those. She walked into the kitchen and examined the tissue under the light above the sink. Jenna had seen this sort of thing before at her father's clinic. Mr. Morton had brought in his young Rottweiler, Randy, after he'd had a terrible fight with a skunk. She also remembered Mrs. Duncan and her cat, Petunia, who was brought to the clinic after being bitten by a raccoon.

Both animals had foamed at the mouth just like Biscuit, but there was a reason for that—the others had been infected with rabies. They both had bite wounds, from where the virus was transmitted. Biscuit, on the other hand had no visible markings on him—at least none that Jenna saw.

She looked again at the tissue. It was damp with saliva but there was something else on it. Red blotches were splattered throughout the drool. *Oh no . . . blood . . .*

Jenna knew that Biscuit was a healthy dog. He was at her father's clinic a month ago, after he got too friendly with a hornet's nest. Biscuit was always getting into trouble, but he was definitely up to date on his vaccinations. *Maybe the foam is from another animal. But why was he going to attack me? This doesn't make any sense,* she thought.

She remembered what her father had said about Calvin's symptoms; rabies was one of the diseases he mentioned. Jenna wondered if the two were related. She pulled out a small plastic bag from one of the kitchen drawers and placed the tissue inside of it. Her father would need to see this. She placed the baggie in the sink and covered it with a bowl so that none of the four-legged family members would get at it.

The lights were still on inside the clinic. Jenna hoped that Calvin was okay. Turning off all of the downstairs lights, she then headed for her room. Now, she was tired.

When she reached the top of the stairs, she saw that her grandmother's bedroom door was slightly ajar. Usually she slept with the door closed. Jenna thought it might be wise to check on her, so she poked her head into the room. Although it was dark, she could see that the bed was still made and the room was empty. *Grandma probably went over to help Mom and Dad.*

With that final thought, Jenna turned towards her bedroom. Ted and Tony were now inside asleep on the bed. "Boy, you guys are fast!" She took off her robe and slippers, meandered around their curled-up bodies and climbed beneath the sheets. She was once again relegated to the outskirts of the mattress, where she laid down her weary head and went to sleep.

IT'S REINING CATS AND DOGS

Jenna's alarm sounded when the clock stuck eight the next morning. Without looking, she whacked the machine with her hand. "I'm up, I'm up—I hear you," she mumbled into the pillow. Limb by limb, her body slowly lifted. Covering her eyes, she squinted at the sun's rays sparkling through the window. Her bed now felt empty, spacious. Ted and Tony had already left the room.

Her stomach rumbled; she was quite hungry. She put on her robe and slippers, much like the night before, and headed downstairs towards the fridge.

When she arrived at the kitchen, her family was sitting at the table discussing the previous night's events.

"Good morning, did we wake you?" her mother said.

"No, my stomach woke me up, I think."

"Do you want me to make you something, dear?" her grandmother said, smiling.

"I think I'll just have cereal. Thanks, though." Jenna scoured the cupboards. "You guys were up pretty late last night," she said, hopping onto the counter to eat her breakfast.

"Reid, what happened after I went to bed?" her grandmother said.

Jenna's father walked over to the coffee pot and rubbed his eyes. Heading back to the table, he poured three cups and took a sip of one. "Mr. Winters' concerns were justified. Calvin's very sick. He was aggressive and tried to bite everyone. It took all three of us to hold him down. He had a fever, his eyes were dilated and he vomited a number of times while we were holding him. His stool was loose, there was blood and tissue inside of it." He shook his head and furrowed his brow. "I also felt several lumps near his abdomen."

"Oh my God!" Jenna gasped.

"I couldn't believe it either. The symptoms match the diseases, though—rabies, distemper and leukemia. Barbara took all the samples to Nick at the lab downtown. Poor guy, I woke him up and asked him to meet her there around three-thirty in the morning. He knows it's a rush job. I'm just waiting for him to call with some of the results."

He crossed the kitchen to look out the window. "That cat was in perfect health—I gave him the shots myself. If I were more awake right now, I'd probably be losing it. I'm still the new guy in town and I'm responsible for this."

Jenna's mother stood to console him. "Reid, something else is at play here. This is not a case of improper vaccinations, or lack of care. It's something much bigger. Whatever is happening to Calvin is rare and inexplicable. Don't blame yourself. You'll figure this one out. You just need a little time."

"Calvin doesn't have time. If this is what I think it is, then I need to do something about it *now*."

She looked over at the telephone. "What do you want me to do?"

"Make the call," he said.

"Okay." She picked up the phone and dialled a number. "Yes, hello. Susan Baker, please . . ." She waited a moment. "Hi Susan—it's Barbara. I need to cancel the flight. No, it's an emergency, unfortunately. Thank you for helping us book it but we have to cancel. I understand. Thanks again."

"You're not going?" Jenna said. "But you booked this vacation months ago. Aren't there other clinics that could help Calvin?"

"We can't leave, Jenna. This is serious—your father is needed here and I'm going to stay and help him. And I won't be going in to work since I already have the time off."

Jenna's grandmother lifted herself from the chair. "Where is Calvin now? I would like to see him."

"Mom, I don't think that's a good idea right now. Calvin's inside the clinic, but he's finally sleeping."

"Barbara—I want to see him. Besides, he won't even know that I'm there. I'll be truly quiet."

Jenna's father stepped in front of the kitchen door and opened it. "It's all right, Abby. I need to go out there anyway and check on him."

She nodded and headed out the door as he followed behind.

"Jenna, your dad and I are very tired. We were up all night with Calvin. We need things to be quiet today. Take your grandmother to the museum, the two of you can go see that new exhibit."

Jenna complied. "Okay, Mom. I'll get ready right after I finish breakfast."

"Thank you," she said, lowering her coffee cup into the sink. "Wait a minute—what's this?"

"Oh, yeah . . . I totally forgot. It's something that I found last night."

Her mother grunted. "This isn't another one of your science experiments, is it, Jenna? Because I'm still recovering from your last one."

"No, Mom, it isn't. Although your reaction last time was completely worth it," she said with a tweak.

"All right, dear, you had your fun, I'm glad that my high-pitched screaming amused you so. But next time, warn me when you're going to put a tarantula in the bathtub. I almost had a heart attack."

"And the Academy Award goes to my mom for best actress in a dramatic role."

"You'd just better get moving before I make you do the dishes," she smiled.

Jenna jumped off of the counter and ran towards the hallway. "I'm going . . . I'm going . . . but don't throw out that stuff in the sink. It's for Dad. He needs to see it."

She finished off the bowl of cereal as she neared the top of the stairs. Then she paused. *Why was Grandma Abby asking about what happened last night?* Jenna had assumed that with her grandmother's bed being empty, she was out helping her parents at the clinic. But now she questioned her late night whereabouts.

Jenna marched towards the bathroom and placed the bowl on the sink. She leaned over the bathtub to turn on the taps. Warm water burst into her hands as the excitement of the day's events began to mount. The only lingering concern she had was for Calvin.

Once the tub was filled, she turned off the water and prepared for a quick but soothing bath.

* * *

Side by side, the two adults watched as Calvin's belly rose and fell. He was sound asleep when the clinic phone rang. Jenna's father hurried over to pick it up. He listened to the voice on the other end and said, "The paperwork's inside the house—I'll call you right back. Thanks, Nick." He hung up the phone and headed to the house.

Jenna's grandmother moved in for a closer look. She stared at the feline inside the small, padded cage. Her gaze then drifted to the ceiling. Slowly, she closed her eyes.

* * *

Inside the kitchen, Jenna's father had the phone to his ear. Nick was explaining his findings.

"Yeah, that's exactly what I thought. Thanks for getting back to me so soon. Sorry to make you work early, Nick. I'll call if anything changes."

Jenna's mother stood by the counter, concentrating on her husband's half of the conversation. She poured a cup of coffee and handed it to him. "What's the verdict, Reid?"

He took a sip as he hung up the phone. "Nick says that Calvin's red *and* white blood cell count is really low. It could mean both leukemia and distemper. I don't understand—that cat shouldn't be sick, Barbara. He just shouldn't. This is all wrong! These diseases came on too fast—*too fast*!"

"What about the stool sample?"

"There was intestinal lining in the sample which is understandable—if he had distemper. I need to call Mrs. Wightman and have her bring Hershey over. She didn't come by last night and I need to examine him. If there are any more animals with these symptoms, then something needs to be done about it immediately."

His words stopped just as the kitchen door opened. Jenna's grandmother walked into the room with all three dogs following closely behind. She grabbed some treats from one of the cupboards, gave each dog a few and sent them on their way.

As she leaned over to pet Charlie, he turned and barked at her, nearly grasping one of her fingers. She backed away from him and stood by the fridge.

"Charlie, down!" Jenna's father yelled.

Jenna's mother ran over and took a hold of his collar. "Charlie—stop that!"

Still, he continued to bark.

But with one stern look from Jenna's grandmother, the attack was circumvented. Charlie tore out of the kitchen and whimpered all the way to the family room.

"What is going on with everyone? Are you okay, Mom?"

"Oh yes, I'm fine, Barbara," she said, crossing her arms. "Dogs are just funny sometimes, aren't they?"

"Yes, but I've never seen Charlie act like that before . . ."

All three dogs reappeared in the room as each one scratched at the kitchen door to be let out.

With a warming touch, Jenna's father bent down and petted them. Charlie's tongue now dangled happily from his open mouth. "It's okay, boys. Everything's just fine." He stood and opened the door. All three dogs immediately dashed outside.

"He probably just wanted his food, is all," Jenna's grandmother said. Her tone was soft, respectful. "Dogs sometimes get defensive about their food, you know that. Don't blame him."

After that, she left the kitchen.

Jenna was exiting the bathroom when she saw her grandmother coming up the stairs. "Grandma, how did Calvin look?"

She placed her hand on the railing. "He's going to be fine. You don't have to worry."

Her grandmother's face seemed thinner, paler. "Grandma, are you okay?"

She turned away and opened the door to her room. "Yes, dear—I'm all right. I just need a warm bath to get me started."

Jenna stood in the hallway watching her grandmother. There was something off about her gait. She wasn't moving with her normal flamboyant flaunt.

"Grandma?"

"Yes, dear," she stopped.

"I'm going to the museum today to see that new exhibit. We're going together, right?"

Her grandmother half-turned and winked. "Yes, Jenna, that's the plan." She then disappeared into her room.

Jenna was excited. She was looking forward to seeing this new display. With that thought in mind, she darted into her bedroom to prepare herself for the excursion.

ANOTHER PUZZLE PIECE

"Mrs. Wightman's going to bring Hershey over right now," Jenna's father said, hanging up the kitchen telephone.

"That's good, Reid," Jenna's mother said. "We need to see that cat."

Looking down at the sink, he gawked. "What's this, Barbara?"

"Oh, that's Jenna's. She wanted you to see it."

He removed the bowl and picked up the baggie. "Jenna, can you come down here?" he shouted.

A moment later, Jenna ran into the room. "Yeah, Dad, is something wrong?"

He looked at the red-blotted tissue swimming in the baggie. "What's this?"

"It's something I found this morning. I went outside and Biscuit was in the bushes out front."

He rolled his eyes, "I see, and what was Biscuit up to this time?"

Jenna shook her head. "No, Dad. Biscuit was acting really strange. I think he was trying to get inside the house. There were scratches on the windowpane and thick drool on the glass. I know that Biscuit drools a lot anyway, but this was different. He was ferocious—he tried to attack me. But something distracted him, and he took off like a bandit."

Her father was deep in thought. To break the silence, Jenna asked, "Is Calvin still sleeping?"

His response was somewhat delayed. "Yes . . . Calvin is still sleeping . . . he needs to rest. Jenna, did Biscuit have any bite marks or scratches on him, any signs that he'd been in a fight with another animal?"

"Not that I could tell, but it was really dark. It was about three-thirty in the morning—I couldn't see much out there. But from what I saw, he looked okay. Except he was limping when he ran away."

Her father lifted the phone. "And it was definitely Biscuit that you saw?"

"Yes, it was definitely Biscuit. I'd know him anywhere."

He dialled a number and waited. "Hi there, Tommy, it's Dr. Matthews. Is your mom there? Okay, sport, I'll wait . . . Hey, Debra, how are you? Yes . . . well . . . Jenna was just telling me that we had a visit from Biscuit early this morning."

Jenna could hear laughing on the other end of the phone.

"Yes, he is a curious one but my concern is actually for Biscuit. Jenna said that he was acting very aggressive towards her where perhaps, something might be wrong. I was hoping you'd be able to bring him by this afternoon for a check-up, no charge. I'm just wondering about something. Has he been acting differently towards your family at all? How about right now, is he nearby? Oh, he's sleeping. Okay then. Yes, anytime this afternoon would be fine. See you soon."

He hung up the phone and looked at Jenna. "This happened at what time, again?"

"Around three-thirty—I guess just after Mom left with the samples. You and Grandma were outside with Calvin. I didn't want to bother you with it, so I saved it for today."

"Grandma wasn't with us, Jenna. She went to bed right after you did."

"Really? That's weird because her bed was . . . well . . . nothing. Nevermind. So, is there a problem with Biscuit, Dad?"

He didn't answer. Jenna once again, had the feeling that she was being kept in the dark.

"Did you come into contact with him at all?" he asked.

"No, not at all."

"Good," he said. "Because it sounds like Biscuit might be very sick."

THE MUSEUM

On the day that Jenna turned sixteen, she was off in pursuit of her driver's licence. Wheels. Independence. Wind in her hair kind of freedom. It wasn't a revolutionary concept by any means but still she wanted it. First, she needed the practice.

She climbed into the driver's seat of her mother's car and squealed. "I love driving!" Her feet did a happy dance as her grandmother closed the passenger side door.

"Now, it's just like the last time. Look around before you back out of the driveway."

Jenna reversed carefully, then put the car into 'drive' and headed down the road. She was dripping with excitement. This was her fifth time behind the wheel, and each experience had left her wanting more. Her enthusiasm gradually dissipated however, as questions about her grandmother's strange disappearance the night before popped into her head.

"Grandma, where did you go last night? I was up at three-thirty in the morning and you weren't there. Dad said that you weren't with them either. I was worried about you."

"I'm sorry you were worried, Jenna, but I couldn't sleep. I went for a walk." Her words were camouflaged by the weird smile she was wearing.

Jenna was mystified by her grandmother's response. Back in Salem, that would have been normal. Her grandmother was a true night owl and loved walking at all hours. But since they'd moved to Wichita, she hadn't done that sort of thing. When she wasn't travelling, she remained close to the house. No late night walks. Not even one.

"You should be careful," Jenna said. "I saw on the news that there might be a wild cat loose in the area. It's been coming around after dark. The newsman also said that thirty people have gone missing in Wichita—did you know that?"

Her grandmother remained quiet.

Jenna glanced over at Tommy's house as they passed by it. Biscuit was asleep on the front lawn. "Biscuit seems better. You should have seen him earlier, though. He was acting crazy."

"Don't worry—he won't bother you again."

Jenna was stunned by the confidence in her grandmother's affirmation. "How do you know that?"

"Well, Biscuit's going to your father's clinic today to be examined. He'll be in good hands. And just like that," she said, snapping her fingers, "he'll be back to normal. Believe me, your father will take care of everything."

"I sure hope so," Jenna said, checking the rear view mirror. "He's such a sweet dog. I wouldn't want anything bad to happen to him."

Minutes later, they arrived at the Lionhead Museum. "We're here!" Jenna cried. She bounced out of the car and hurried over to help her grandmother out. Then together, they made their way towards the front doors of the museum. Jenna was thrilled when she saw the large golden lion proudly perched above the doors. It could have been her millionth visit to the museum and still she'd have the same reaction.

As Jenna approached the doors, she had a sneaking suspicion that her grandmother was hesitating. "Are you okay?" she asked.

"Oh yes, I'm fine. My bones are just a little sore today, Jenna. I need to take my time, that's all. Give me an hour and I'll be hopping around like you," she grinned.

Jenna opened one of the heavy glass doors to let her grandmother walk through. She followed behind and then headed over to the front desk.

A big, "Hello," resonated through the front hall. It was Anna, the secretary. "Abby, Jenna! How are you ladies doing?"

"We're good," Jenna answered. "And you?"

"Oh, I'm excited. Did your mother tell you that we have a new exhibit opening today in the Egyptian wing?"

"Yes, we're here to see it. She told us about it yesterday, although she was a little fuzzy on the details," Jenna said.

Anna crossed her arms and looked around the hall. "Yes, I know. They didn't tell us much about it until this morning. I'll be going up there shortly to see it. By the way, did your mom and dad make it to the airport all right? I can't believe that they're finally going to Spain! I'm so jealous," she laughed.

"Well, actually, an emergency came up at my dad's clinic and they had to cancel the trip. Mom's helping him until it gets resolved. I'm sure she'll be in touch with you soon."

Anna frowned. "I'm so sorry. I know how much they wanted to go."

"Yeah, they booked the trip months ago. But that's okay, they'll still go. Just not now is all."

Anna looked down at her watch. "Oh boy, I better get back to work. Maybe I'll give your mom a quick call later. So, you know where you're going then, right, Jenna?"

"Yes, thank you."

"It was nice to see you, Abby," Anna smiled.

"You as well," she returned.

Jenna turned and led the way towards the escalators.

They boarded the moving stairs and rode them to the second floor. Jenna's eyes widened when she saw the large banner advertising the new display. *'Share In The Mystery. Bring Your Imagination. Feel The Magic. See The Mummy!'*

"Mom said something about a mummy but she didn't have much to go on."

When they stepped off the escalator, her grandmother paused. "I'm going to visit the Thailand exhibit first. I'll meet up with you after. You go on ahead to the new exhibit." She turned quickly and walked away before Jenna could say anything.

Jenna watched as she left. Her grandmother's behaviour seemed a bit off, but how exactly, she couldn't quite pinpoint. Besides, her mind was focused on the room down the hall. With a jubilant buzz, she headed for her destination.

After a short hike past a lengthy dinosaur mural, Jenna entered a room with ivory-coloured walls and soft citron lighting. The ambiance was serene, soothing. Her outer elation was calmed by its effect.

The first thing she noticed was a large rectangular display case in the centre of the room. Her eyes were immediately drawn to it. She approached slowly. The case was made of thick sheets of glass. It stood roughly ten feet high and was nearly eight feet wide. Jenna was stunned by the size of it. She was also surprised to see thick metal bars surrounding it. *What's that all about?* she wondered. *I guess they didn't want anyone getting into it.*

Jenna moved as close as she could to the display, so not to miss a single detail. She looked through the metal bars and stopped. "Wow—this is amazing!"

Inside the case was a large, decorated wooden coffin. The colours were brilliant. The head of the coffin was shaped like a cat and the body was shaped like a human. Jenna was impressed by the amount of delicate detail.

Lying next to the coffin was an intricately wrapped, linen-covered outline of a cat's body. "Oh my God!" Jenna gasped. She had seen mummies before, many of them in fact, but this one was completely different. This was the biggest cat mummy that she had ever seen. It looked like an enlarged lion. Its body was tightly woven within the old white linen. It was so clear: every angle, every point, every curve.

Jenna examined the mummy carefully. It was odd, but in some strange way, it seemed alive to her. That after three thousand years of rest it was somehow, in some form, still alive. She was entranced. Her eyes were captivated, lured into the case.

She stared at the mummy for quite some time, as if she had no will of her own. Her gaze broke when she heard a whisper. Begrudgingly, she shifted her eyes from the case to search the room. No one was there. She stepped back from the display and listened carefully. *It must be the air conditioning or something,* she thought. Her focus returned to the case.

Surrounding the mummy, were four sand-coloured jars, each capped with a brightly-designed animal head. A darkened sheet of paper read: *'These Canopic jars were used to preserve the internal organs of this cat. The stomach, intestines, liver and lungs were removed and stored for safekeeping for its journey into the afterlife.'*

Jenna was fascinated. She wanted to touch and feel everything for herself. Her hand reached through the bars. With her fingers only inches away from the glass, a voice behind her thundered, "Don't touch that!"

Her heart trembled as she spun around.

Facing her now, was her grandmother. She looked terror-stricken. "Please don't touch that—it's not safe."

"Grandma—you scared me!" she said, clenching her chest. "What's wrong? It's just glass."

"I'm sorry, Jenna, you just shouldn't. Besides, you know that you're not supposed to touch the cases. And this one is very special. If you were to touch the glass, a security alarm would go off and you wouldn't want that."

Looking back at the mummy, Jenna shuddered. "Why is there so much security for this? Wait a minute . . . how did you know about the alarm?" When she peered back at her grandmother, she was gone. For a moment, Jenna thought that her eyes and ears were playing tricks on her.

Then her grandmother poked her head out from behind another display. "I'm over here," she said.

Jenna walked towards the voice, now feeling a little disturbed.

Her grandmother was sitting on a bench. "Jenna, do you mind if I take the car and go home? I don't seem to be feeling that well. I don't want you to leave on account of me. I know that you're enjoying your visit, but I have to go."

Kneeling down, she nodded. "Of course—I'll drive you home."

"No, dear, I'll be fine. You stay here," she insisted.

"Okay, Grandma. You take the car and I'll walk back. I'll see you at home later."

Jenna escorted her grandmother out of the museum and helped her into the vehicle. She didn't like seeing her unwell, it was unnatural. For as long as Jenna had known her, she was a fit, healthy, active person. She walked, danced, cooked, explored, travelled. Her grandmother was very spry. Although her sixty-fifth birthday was approaching, Jenna still regarded her as a youth. The entire family constantly referred to her as 'the senior teen'—a term she found quite endearing.

Jenna watched as the car rolled out of the parking lot. She decided to leave the museum and follow her grandmother on foot. Her well-being was more important right now.

* * *

As Jenna neared her house, the air began to move. She heard something on the road behind her. Pivoting in place, she witnessed the joyful performance of a dancing newspaper.

Then, everything got dark.

The sun disappeared and the warm air cooled as a thick lining of clouds swept over the street. Jenna knew that it was only a matter of minutes before the rain started.

She raced off towards her house but still felt like she was being followed. Looking back, she saw the prancing paper chasing her down the street. Spinning on her heels, she reached out and grabbed it. Her eyes caught a glimpse of the front headline as the pages wiggled between her fingers. '*Feline Mummy Arrives at Museum.*' Jenna smiled.

Suddenly, lightning pierced the air. Frightened by the terrifying sound, Jenna dropped the paper. She turned in the direction of home but was startled by a large animal that was moving towards her. Immediately, she ceased all movement as it approached. Although she was overwhelmed with both fear and fascination, she remained stiff as a statue.

The outline of the animal looked like a cat. Jenna's mind quickly registered the image as she compared the body to that of a king-sized panther. Although her fondness of felines was unquestionable, Jenna realized that the figure that stood before her most likely did not possess the same affinity for humans as its domestic relatives.

As the animal closed in, it gazed upon her with crimson eyes. She dared not move for fear of waking up to either a dream or a nightmare.

Another flash of lightning lit the sky and the animal's eyes grew large. Jenna's vision filled with red. She closed her eyes and then opened them only to find that the animal had disappeared, and the newspaper was now in its place.

Jenna crept carefully towards it. She looked in all directions, searching for the cat. It was nowhere in sight. With jittery fingers she picked up the paper. The black and white print was all gone, the pages were completely bare.

Lightning struck again as waves of thunder shook the ground. Jenna dropped the paper and ran.

Nothing could catch up to her now.

GRANDMA ABBY

Jenna's legs were moving so fast that she couldn't see them anymore. She scrambled up the front porch stairs, swung open the door and collapsed on the other side of it.

A low growl came from outside, entering through the cracks in the frame. Jenna wasn't sure whether it was the wind or not. With her back pressed against the door, she attempted to catch her breath.

Then, something clawed at the other side. To Jenna, it felt like sharp nails pawing at the wood. Her face went pale. Something was trying to get in.

She sat motionless on the floor, too afraid to move. Her body was still, a tactic similar to bear evasion. *Go away—just go away!* she pleaded.

Moments later, the scratching ceased. *Okay, get a grip,* she told herself. *It was probably just a broken branch.*

Gravity kicked in when she uprooted her body to regain composure. She peered through the glass beside the door, not knowing what to expect. Scanning the yard, she saw nothing. A giggle erupted from her mouth when she realized how ridiculous she looked, hiding from the wind.

When she turned towards the stairs, she screamed. "Ahh!"

Her grandmother was now standing in front of her.

"Grandma—you scared me. Again!" she said, tapping her chest.

"I'm so sorry, Jenna. Are you okay? I didn't mean to frighten you."

Suddenly, a gust of wind blew open the door. Jenna jumped at the sound. "This is crazy!" Quickly, she threw herself at the door, slamming it shut, locking it.

She looked over at her grandmother who was holding the banister. "That's quite the storm we're having. Are you all right? You've had a lot of scares today."

There was a silent pause, then both women broke out into laughter.

Jenna shook her head. "When did I become such a scaredy-cat?"

Her grandmother grinned. "Tell you what, I'm feeling much better now. Why don't you go dry off, and then come down and help me make some of my homemade white cocoa pudding cookies. Besides, I have a story to tell you."

Jenna was intrigued. "What kind of story?"

"One that you won't soon forget," she said with a lifted brow.

"Okay—I'll be right back." Jenna charged up the stairs.

As she settled into dry clothes, she thought about her grandmother's flare for the dramatics. Every part of her body was used to interpret her experiences, from the wrinkles in her forehead to the coloured polish on her toes. No story was safe from her eccentricities.

Jenna headed down the stairs to the kitchen, where her grandmother awaited her with a cup of raspberry tea.

"Let's start baking," she said.

"Grandma, are you sure you're up for this?"

"Oh, yes. After I left the museum, I felt better. I even picked up some groceries on the way home. I'm sorry—I didn't mean to worry you."

"It's okay." Jenna looked down at her wristwatch. "I guess Mom and Dad are still busy at the clinic. I wonder what's going on in there."

"I don't know, but I'm sure your parents have it all under control. Let's just stay out of their way, shall we."

"So, you have another story to tell me," Jenna probed.

"Yes, I do," she said, turning on the oven.

"I'm all ears."

Her grandmother looked on with twinkly eyes. "First, the cookies."

Together, they stirred the ingredients and then placed the dough into small mounds on the cookie sheets. Jenna loved baking. She loved it even more when she was with her grandmother.

After the cookies were in the oven, they sat down at the kitchen table to enjoy their cups of tea. Patiently, Jenna waited for the entertainment to begin.

"There once was an ancient city in the land of Siam. It was known as Menao," her grandmother started. "Nine large, powerful Siamese cats guarded the small and humble city. The cats were placed at the city's edges, surrounding the people who lived there. In the centre was a temple for King Odon, the King of the Cats. It was where the people would go to worship." She held the cup of tea in her hands as she spoke.

"The nine guardians were loved by the gods. Each one wore a ruby medallion around its neck as a royal seal and protective talisman. Without its ruby, each cat would be vulnerable. And without all nine cats, the city would be left unprotected. The people of Menao knew this, and so the cats were never to be touched. The people believed that the cats protected them from all that was evil."

Jenna was captivated. She awaited each new word that escaped her grandmother's lips.

"Anyone who tried to capture or take the cats had a curse placed upon them, an awful curse, Jenna. The gods would demand their eternal souls in return for their crime. Their bodies would be wrapped and sent to an afterlife full of disease and pain." She stopped, looked away and then continued. "And so, Menao was safe."

Jenna demanded more. "What happened next?"

"Well, the people feared the Siamese cats and their power, yet they truly believed that they would be protected by them. Everything remained in balance. As long as the cats were untouched, all was protected."

"Did something happen to the city?"

Her grandmother's tone took a dismal dive. "Menao is now lost, Jenna. One stormy night, four strangers came and stole one of the cats, then disappeared into darkness. The thieves were never captured and the cat remained missing. It was later discovered that the precious medallion was robbed from its neck. The thieves had only wanted to steal the ruby, not the cat. But because of their crime, the city was left vulnerable."

"What happened to the other cats?" Jenna had to know.

"The remaining cats were turned into stone by incantation. Only King Odon's most trusted servants were permitted to touch them. The cats and their medallions were carefully wrapped in dark cloth. They were each taken to the ends of the Earth and hidden by the servants. They gave a sacred oath never to reveal the cats' locations—until the time was needed. But one cat is still missing, the one that was stolen from Menao. Until this cat is returned to its rightful place, a curse remains on anyone that crosses its path. You see, it's searching for its talisman."

Jenna soaked in the words. "Wow, what a story. You were right, that was—"

Her grandmother waved her hand quickly. "Listen to me, this new exhibit at the museum is surrounded by controversy. It's believed that the artefact inside the case is indeed the missing Siamese cat. But there is much trouble with this cat. The fact that it's wrapped in Egyptian cloth, speaks volumes. But as tight as the linens may be, they cannot contain its soul. And that is what has escaped. Anyone who tries to come near it will suffer misfortune."

She glanced around the room, cautiously. "There have been many accidents at the museum already. Accidents that cannot be explained, Jenna. Those who have come into contact with the mummy have disappeared—and not been found. That's why I did not want you to touch the display."

The contorted expression on Jenna's face epitomized her disbelief. "Are you serious? I thought this was just a story."

Her grandmother's voice was firm. "Do not ignore the curse, Jenna. The Siamese Mummy will plague all of us until its ruby talisman—the Star of Omandai—is found and reunited with it. The only way to help it is to find the ruby. Only then, will peace be restored to Menao, and history will be rewritten."

"How come Anna didn't know about this?" Jenna said.

"No one will ever talk about it at the museum, Jenna, because they don't know. Do you understand now? They don't know the true history behind it. They only know what they have been told by false legend. All they know of truth, is that the Siamese Mummy is a rare artefact because it doesn't belong where it is. It's not in its rightful place. You'll soon find that out."

Jenna had no idea where the story ended. Her grandmother had taken on a much graver tone from when she started. Where was the jovial smile and dazzling theatrics that accompanied her tales, Jenna wondered.

In a step towards normalcy, her grandmother stood, opened the oven door and removed the cookies.

Jenna relaxed in her seat. "The cookies smell delicious."

There was no response. Her grandmother's back was facing her when she lifted the cookies off of the pans.

"Grandma, are you okay?"

Slowly, she turned around.

A horrifying jolt brought Jenna to her feet when she realized that the person looking back at her was not the one she knew. "Oh my God!" Frantically, she stumbled backwards.

Her grandmother's eyes were pulsating red as her hands began to morph. Claws were growing from the tips of her fingers just as her body—

"Wake up, Jenna, wake up!" a tender voice spoke.

Jenna's eyes popped open.

"My dear, you were falling asleep. Are you all right?" her grandmother said, touching her hand.

"Grandma!" she said, jerking back her arm. She looked around the kitchen. Her tension was alleviated by familiar surroundings. "Oh no, did I fall asleep? I'm so sorry. I don't know what came over me. I guess I'm just tired."

"It's okay, I'm not offended." She placed a few cookies onto a plate and handed them to her. "You go get some sleep. Take these with you, and don't forget your tea. We need to keep things quiet while your parents are busy working. I'll see you in a little while."

Jenna tossed out a sleepy smile. "Thank you for the cookies." She then left the kitchen and headed for her room.

She was greeted by happy meows. Ted and Tony looked up at her from the bed and purred. Apparently, their nap was over. She settled on the edge of the bedspread and nibbled away at a cookie. Although a delicious and comforting distraction, she felt that there was a more pressing subject at hand: sleep.

A breeze of wind rushed through the window as Jenna and the cats looked over. "I don't remember leaving that open." She disposed of her worry however, as she was too tired to concern herself with something so trivial.

She stood and closed the window, then returned to the bed and ate the last of the cookies. Sip by sip, she washed them down with tea. Her belly was now full and her body was ready to rest. She tucked herself beneath the sheets and positioned her head on the pillow. *What a weird day*, she thought. With that, she closed her eyes and disappeared into slumber.

THE CAT'S MEOW

In a mental torrent, Jenna rolled about, as her mind leapt from dream to dream. Monstrous cats, barking dogs, human screams—all were keeping her from a restful sleep.

She awoke suddenly to the sound of a snarling dog. Slightly troubled by the noise, she listened to locate its whereabouts. It was coming from downstairs. She looked at the alarm clock and grumbled. "Nine o'clock? Oh great—I slept the day away!"

Jenna heard the dog now scratching at the kitchen door to be let out. Quickly, she jumped out of bed and went to her parent's room. The door was half open. She peeked inside and found Sam and Max asleep on the bed. Her mother and father weren't there. *Charlie must be downstairs.*

Charlie was the most protective one of the bunch. The family had come to learn that if he was barking at something, it was serious. He chased away anything that didn't belong on the property, including people.

Tonight, something outside was bothering him.

Jenna hurried back into her room and crept towards the window. Her eyes scoured the yard. First, she saw nothing—only the lights from the clinic. Then, she saw a strange shadow. She couldn't make out what it was, but she knew something was there.

A dark figure stood by the swing set. Her eyes adjusted to its form. Within the reach of the clinic lights, she could see the outline of a broad, robust animal. It moved towards the building, then turned away abruptly and headed in the other direction. It did this a number of times until Jenna finally realized what it was doing: the animal was pacing. It seemed to be keeping its distance from the clinic.

Then she caught full sight of it. "Oh my God!"

Downstairs, Charlie was going crazy.

A low growl echoed through the night air. Jenna's jaw dropped open.

She listened as Charlie backed away from the kitchen door and ran up the stairs to join the other dogs.

Jenna was stunned. *How is this possible? This can't be another dream, it just can't be!* Regardless of her fear-driven skepticism, she wanted to know more. For the moment, her curiosity triumphed over her trepidation.

Slowly, she raised the window. Leaning through the opening, she could now see and hear the animal moving in the grass. Hoping to remain invisible, she watched in silence.

The still air was cut when her hand slipped and she lost her balance. Her body teetered precariously through the opening. She jostled frantically to get back inside, but it was too late—the animal had discovered her.

Instantly, it scaled the house with its eyes. It found Jenna and watched her with a hunter's glare. Its vision glowed red in the dark. It raised its head and unleashed a deep, bellowing roar.

Jenna closed her eyes and opened them only to find that the animal had disappeared into the night. She surveyed the entire yard. *Where did it go?* Closing the window, she ran to her grandmother's room as fast as she could.

When she pushed the door open, she was surprised to see that her grandmother was again, absent. Confused, she headed back to her own room. Just as she was about to step inside, a noise came from the kitchen. It was a sharp, uneasy sound. A dish had been broken.

"What the—"

She made her way towards the stairs and quietly began to descend. Halfway down, she heard her grandmother's voice. Something about it seemed different. It was deep and raspy, much unlike her normal tone. She then observed what appeared to be a thick, black tail moving inside the kitchen.

Jenna sat peeking through the stairway banister. *I don't believe this—this can't be real!*

A voice from the kitchen reached out to her and spoke, "I see you . . ."

Uh oh! Jenna heard something moving towards the hallway. Immediately, she ran back to the safety of her room. The window was now open. She ran across the floor and slammed it shut. Then, as fast as she could, she jumped onto the bed and took refuge beneath the covers. Her pulse was racing. She felt like a certifiable lunatic. For here she was, hiding in her bed, hoping—praying that she wouldn't be attacked by a tail.

It's finally happened, she told herself. *I've cracked—I'm going nuts!*

Her mind began to disintegrate and her body began to weaken as a tremendous pressure fell upon her chest. It was akin to someone sitting on top of her. Jenna had no cares in the world. Her eyes rolled back in her head, and everything went dark. From there, she disappeared into a deep sleep. There were no worries about the animal in the backyard or the tail in the kitchen.

Jenna didn't even seem to mind that she was being watched from inside her very own room.

ANOTHER DAY

The bright sunshine was intoxicating as it glistened through the open window. Jenna stretched her arms and welcomed in the morning rays. With her toes leading the way, she slipped out of bed and sauntered over to the window. She leaned through and saw Charlie sound asleep in the doghouse beside the porch. Sam was chewing on a rubber toy squirrel, and Max was digging a hole by the swing set. She yawned and closed the window.

"Wait a minute—I closed that last night. I know I did!" Her body shivered with fear, knowing that someone had come into her room while she was sleeping. "Oh, for Pete's sake, snap out of it!" she chided herself. "It was probably just Mom or Dad."

She wandered into the hallway towards her grandmother's room to see if she was awake. Opening the door, she sprouted a smile. "Good morning!"

"Well, good morning, Jenna," her grandmother said. She was sitting in bed with her reading glasses on. Perched on her lap, was the morning newspaper. "You sure slept soundly last night. I thought you'd never wake up. How about some of my banana pancakes—are you hungry?"

"I'm Starving!" Jenna loved her grandmother's banana pancakes; they were famous in her family's kitchen. "What about Mom and Dad?"

"Jenna," she said, placing a finger over her mouth, "your parents were up very late again last night. They're still sleeping. Don't worry—we'll make extra for them."

Quiet as mice, they stepped into the hallway. "I'll be down in a minute," her grandmother said.

Jenna continued on down the stairs. She yawned as she strolled through the hallway. Her route was momentarily interrupted when her feet came to a standstill. She swivelled around to face the mirror hanging on the wall. Curiously, she stared at the reflection. Something was unusually different.

Jenna found herself looking at a fading image of an animal behind her. Turning quickly, she saw nothing. When she looked back at the mirror, the image was gone.

"What are you staring at? You look like you've seen a ghost," her grandmother said, appearing behind her.

"Grandma," she said, her voice guarded, "could you tell me more about the Siamese Mummy?"

"Of course, dear."

Together, they walked into the kitchen. "Take a seat. I've got the batter all ready to go. These pancakes are going to be my best yet." She reached across the stove and turned on the burner.

Jenna lowered herself onto one of the chairs. Her brain was intent on learning the truth behind the mummy, and her stomach knew that nothing went better with a good story than homemade banana pancakes.

She watched as her grandmother stirred the batter. "I saw something, Grandma, but I'm not sure if it was real."

"Oh?" she said, pouring the first batch into the frying pan.

"I saw a giant cat on the road yesterday during that storm, or at least I think—"

Her words were stunted as the pan fell from her grandmother's hand. "Ouch!" she cried.

Jenna ran over to help her. "Are you okay? Did you burn your hand?"

Immediately, she withdrew her arm and hid it behind her. "No, I'm fine, dear. Just clumsy, that's all."

Jenna looked into her eyes. "You must be tired—your eyes are bloodshot."

Her grandmother seemed upset by the comment. She stood up and left the kitchen. "I didn't sleep well last night, Jenna. Please, finish the pancakes. I must rest now." The words trailed behind her like a ribbon.

"Of course, I'll take care of everything." Jenna picked up the pan and placed it on the burner. With a damp cloth, she wiped up the floor. Worries clouded her mind as she cooked the remaining batter. Her concern was for her grandmother's hand; she wanted to make sure that she wasn't hurt.

Jenna agonized over the incident until she was finished. Although only sixteen, she had become quite the worry wart. She stressed over many things—even little things that were unimportant. 'Trivial torment', her parents called it. This however, was important. Her brooding was well grounded this time.

Jenna saw that her grandmother had steeped a pot of tea. She poured the brew into a rose-coloured mug, turned off the stove and headed for the stairs.

She inched open her grandmother's door and found her sleeping on top of the sheets. Jenna slinked into the room and placed the mug on the bedside table. She tiptoed across the floor and picked up the blanket that was lying on the rocking chair in the corner. Holding it made her smile. It was Jenna's favourite blanket from her grandmother's house in Salem. It was black with white trim, and had red roses embroidered on it.

Hoping not to disturb her grandmother, she placed the blanket on top of her. At that moment, Jenna saw the markings on her hand. And they weren't small. They were in fact, deep scratches. She leaned over to take a closer look. Jenna thought that her grandmother had burned herself when she dropped the pan, but that wasn't the case at all.

She inspected the room and noticed a half-empty bottle of green liquid sitting atop of the dresser on the other side of the bed.

Silently, she walked over and lifted the bottle to sniff the contents. To Jenna, it smelled like some sort of herbal remedy. She identified cinnamon, cardamom, ginger and rosemary. The rest she couldn't tell. It wasn't medicinal—it was natural. She assumed that it was one of her grandmother's special concoctions.

When she looked back at the scratches, they began to disappear. Jenna didn't blink, she just watched in wonder. She was stupefied by the vanishing act.

Her grandmother slowly opened her eyes and then closed them. "We must find it," she murmured. "I know we are close. Jenna will help."

Jenna's back straightened at the sound of her name. Perhaps her grandmother was dreaming. Whatever the reason, Jenna thought it would be best to leave.

She went downstairs to the kitchen and poured herself a cup of tea. Taking a sip by the window, she sighed. For her, things were just as jumbled and mystifying inside the house as they were outside at the clinic.

Her inner thoughts were soon distracted by Max's digging in the backyard. He was diligently working on a new site. Jenna laughed; even the dog was a paleontologist.

She opened the door and shouted, "Max—stop digging! Do I have to come out there, Mister?" You couldn't tell he was a Golden Retriever by the amount of dirt he was wearing.

Jenna decided to go outside and see what all the fuss was about.

When she approached the brown-covered canine, she realized that he had dug an impressive hole. "Max, what am I going to do with you?"

He looked up at her and licked his lips.

"What did you find this time, bud? A shoe? A stick? Another bone, maybe?" She leaned over and peered into the hole. Max's earth removal had revealed a long, white structure. "Did you bury this?" She smiled and patted him on the head.

The cavity was approximately two feet deep and three feet wide, and inside it, was a bone. It was much too big to belong to a cat or dog. Jenna likened the size to that of a cow.

She wasn't too surprised by the discovery; after all it was a farm. Who knew what family pets or livestock were buried beneath it.

Jenna reached into the hole and felt along the edges. It was a leg bone. She was about to pull out her hand when she felt another bone attached to it. Then another. And another . . .

Her body was halfway into the space when she heard Max barking hysterically behind her.

"Max, calm down!" She sat up and looked around, but saw no cause for the disturbance. He seemed fixated on something by her bedroom window. She gazed up and saw her grandmother standing inside the room. Jenna was momentarily stumped. *Grandma's up, already?*

She shrugged away her care and focussed on the fact that her grandmother was feeling better. "Oh, Max—it's just Grandma. You're being silly."

A butterfly went fluttering by and off he went in pursuit. "Boy, talk about short attention spans," she laughed.

She directed her concentration back to the hole. The bones appeared to be rather big. "I wonder what this is." Jenna wanted to dig further into the ground. In order to do this, she would need a shovel. The basement was where she would find it.

She hiked back to the house and went down the stairs to the lowest floor. Turning on the light, she browsed around the space. Organized on the table in the centre of the room, was a large collection of broken fossil pieces. Scattered around the fossils, were numerous chipped and unwanted artefacts that had been discarded from the museum. Surrounding the table, were hordes of tools, as well as cages and equipment for her father's clinic.

Jenna found a small shovel hanging on the wall with a larger one leaning against it. She picked up the big shovel and headed back outside to the hole.

She started digging around the bones, further into the ground. She was very careful not to disturb any of them. With each scoop of the shovel, she unearthed more of the puzzle. Her mind was stimulated, her senses inflamed with curiosity. Her canine catalyst had incited this subterranean quest—and Jenna was quite glad that he had.

For hours she sat, uncovering bone after bone. Once finished, she brushed away the remaining dirt with her hands. An entire skeleton was now staring back at her. "Wow—this is amazing!"

"Jenna, what are you doing out there?" a voice called from the house.

She turned and saw her mother standing by the kitchen door.

"Nothing. I'm just helping Max with something."

"Well, come inside. Your dad and I need to talk to you for a minute."

"Okay, I'll be right there." Jenna wanted to examine the skeleton further, but didn't think it was a good idea to bother her parents with it. And more importantly, she didn't want the dogs near the bones. The picnic blanket would make a good cover, she figured. It had been left outside from the other night, folded up by the swing set.

Jenna grabbed the fabric and spread it over the hole. She found some rocks behind the swings and placed them on each of the corners. "That should be fine until I get back," she said, happy with her decision.

When she entered the kitchen, her parents were devouring the pancakes. Her father sipped his tea and looked up. "Jenna, your mom and I have a lot of work to do today. We've got more animals to examine and more people to talk to. We're going to be very busy at the clinic. We don't have time for anything else."

"Okay. How's everyone doing out there?"

He frowned. "Calvin and Hershey are pretty sick. Oddly enough—Biscuit seems to be fine. It doesn't make any sense. He did have rabies, but then a few hours later, his symptoms disappeared." He took a sip from his mug. "Biscuit's going to be fine but I don't know what's going to happen to the others. I can't understand why he's the only one improving."

"Maybe cats are less immune to what's going on," Jenna guessed.

"Maybe," he said. "Hell—I don't even know what's going on. Nick said that veterinary clinics all over Wichita are being inundated with sick animals. I've got two more dogs coming in today and seven cats. I'm going to keep as many animals at the clinic as I can. Diseased animals are showing up all over the place, which means that this is no longer, random. Not anymore."

"Dad, is there anything I can do?"

"In a little while, your mom will be going into town for some supplies. I'll be working at the clinic. We must not be disturbed, Jenna. Everyone's got to stay out of our way. If we need anything, we'll let you know."

Jenna's father was normally a relaxed man, but right now he looked absolutely frazzled.

"Okay, Dad." Jenna hoisted a couple of pancakes onto a plate and drowned them in maple syrup. "I'll be around though, so let me know if you need anything." With her food and fork in hand, she headed to her room.

Sitting on her bed, she ate her breakfast. *What is going on around here?* First, Calvin, Hershey and Biscuit were sick. Now, many animals in the city were sick. *What's going to happen to them?* She thought about all the human disappearances and wondered if they were somehow linked to their four-legged counterparts.

What she really wanted though, was to go outside and look at the skeleton, but she didn't want to draw any attention to it. When the time was right, she would tell her mother about it and ask for her help. But right now, her parents had more important things to do.

Jenna tried to wrap her mind around the bones. Ultimately, she decided to consult one of her biology textbooks. From the shelf above the desk, she pulled out a book and flipped to the section on skeletal anatomy.

Her eyes bulged and her pulse began to quicken. "You've got to be kidding me!" In less than a second, she dropped the book and ran out of the room.

One of the images she found was an exact pictorial replica of the skeleton that Max had uncovered. Jenna needed to see it again to confirm it.

She flew down the stairs and sprinted out into the backyard. In a flash, she looked around. *Good, no one's here.* Carefully, she removed the picnic blanket. The head, the body, the tail of the animal—all of the bones were there. The skeleton was large, bigger than that of a lion, she estimated. "I don't believe it!"

She sat down by the skull and stared at the canine teeth. They were long and gleaming white, like they hadn't been used for anything. The entire skeleton was clean and impeccably unstained.

Jenna was astounded by the size of it. Even its foot bones and tail vertebrae were larger than normal. She was confounded by the whole discovery. Her family had moved to the farm a year ago, and yet the skeleton was found only today. And everything was intact; no bones were missing or broken.

Jenna stood to analyse the situation. "It must have been buried quickly, and recently, too. But . . . that's not possible. If the bones were just buried, then how come we didn't see it happen?"

She took a step back. Something wasn't right. To Jenna, it felt like the skeleton was moving, somehow. She had an irrepressible feeling that the animal lying in the ground was not quite dead. Yet, in a strange, inexplicable way, it enthralled her.

She decided to stay by its side.

As the day progressed, Jenna remained outside with the bones. So fixated was her mind, that she hadn't noticed the sun setting.

One of the dogs barked and she looked over at the house. Checking her watch, she gasped. It was already eight-thirty. "I'd better get something to eat." She stood and removed the dirt from her clothes. The refrigerator was summoning her.

Although she didn't want to leave, she needed food to continue. She disengaged her focus and reluctantly followed the growls of her stomach. As she left, a frosty shiver slid up her body. It wasn't a chill from the onset of night air. It was a prickly message, reminding her to return.

And shrouded in secrecy, the messenger waited.

OUT THERE

Twenty minutes later, Jenna was sitting on the back porch stairs, munching on a peanut butter and jelly sandwich. The sun had set and the moon was about to take its place, when Jenna noticed something sprawled out next to the swing set.

"Sammy, is that you?" she called. It was sometimes difficult to see him at night, considering how his black coat camouflaged him. "Come here, Sammy, it's time to go inside!"

The figure remained still in place. Sam always responded to a call, so Jenna ruled him out. It was getting darker by the minute and she was starting to get nervous. With all of the unexpected visitors recently, it could be anything. "Max? Charlie?"

Jenna couldn't see what she was looking at, and the lights behind the clinic blinds were just beyond its reach.

Her mind was drawn to the concealed figure. She stood up and walked down the stairs towards it. The wind began to pick up as the distance between them lessened. Jenna felt the first drop of rain on her forehead, and then she stopped. Two red eyes glared back at her. She recognized them immediately.

Like a beehive buzzing with activity, her brain was swarming with questions. "Who are you? What do you want? Why are you here?"

The animal responded with an irritated growl. Instantly, Jenna awoke from her trance. The animal's mouth slowly opened, exposing its long, pointed fangs. It then turned and with a steady gait, walked towards the cornfield.

"Wait—" she said, running after it.

Moments later, it disappeared into the stalks.

Jenna stopped and looked down at her feet. She was standing next to the hole that she and Max had dug. The picnic blanket had been removed, and the skeleton that they had unearthed was now gone.

A booming bellow came from inside the cornfield. For some unknown reason, Jenna was compelled to follow it. With prudent steps, she made her way to the edge of the yard.

Reaching the field, she stopped and looked into the vast array of stalks that stood before her. Deep breaths penetrated her system as each prepared her body for an unknown journey. Then, with a momentous heave, she pushed herself on. "Ready or not, here I come."

KING OF THE CATS

Through the voluminous maze of green stalks, she moved. It seemed as though she'd been wandering for hours, when in reality it was only minutes. She held her hands out in front of her, pushing the leaves aside as she blindly felt her way through the dark field. Invigorated by the promise of exploration, she continued on. Her pulse accelerated with each step; her body was truly alive. Her senses held fast to the sounds of the animal ahead of her.

Jenna knew that she was being led into another world; what she was doing was not natural. But her mind was curious and her nerves were strong.

The ground beneath her feet began to soften, and with the next few steps, she felt it loosen. Closing her eyes, she breathed in her surroundings. Her vision of the animal had departed but still she focused on its location. When she opened her eyes, the cornfield had disappeared. All that existed was white desert sand and infinite black sky.

The moon was a ghostly ball of ivory light, casting its glow onto the darkness around her. The stars twinkled brightly above in a sea of onyx air.

She looked ahead and saw something shining before her. It was some sort of large star, dangling low in the sky. Jenna decided to follow the light.

Imprinted in the sand below, was a trail of paw prints leading off into the distance. She followed the impressions as her feet moved alongside the path.

And then she saw it. Up ahead, lay the figure of the animal. Its legs were extended out in a royal and noble manner. Its posture reminded Jenna of the great Sphinx. She could see its chest breathing heavily as it stretched out its body. Its head was poised with majestic dignity. This was the first time that Jenna had seen the animal in its entirety. She clearly saw the contours of a large, powerful cat.

Its beauty was striking. The body was walnut-coloured and sleek, with mighty muscles hidden beneath its coat. Strong, milky jaws sat perched above the feet. And a long, thick tail thrust about behind it. Its nose, ears, paws and tail had all been dipped in black, which was a sharp contrast to the rest of its body.

From nose to tail, this animal exuded nothing but grace and power. Jenna was blown away by its stunning appearance and also by the size. Not only was it a Siamese cat, it was a giant one.

It watched her with fiery red eyes. Jenna didn't move; her body was anchored to the earth.

The animal raised its head and roared into the night sky. It looked back at her and stared. Jenna had no idea what it wanted from her.

Then calmly, it stood and turned away.

"Where are you going?" she yelled out.

The cat disappeared into a large structure behind it.

Jenna shook her head in surprise. An enormous sapphire pyramid sparkled in the night. It was deep ocean-blue and smooth, like glass. "I can't believe I'm seeing this."

She spotted the opening where the Siamese cat had entered. A soft orange glow came from within. Without hesitation, she made her way towards the pyramid.

As she approached, caution caught up with her. *Wait—what am I getting myself into?* But it was too late to turn back. The warm ambiance of the building was reeling her in.

Stepping inside, Jenna was immediately humbled by her surroundings. Directly in front of her, was a statue of stone, built of mammoth proportions. It was a gigantic cat, painted in black and white, and ornately decorated with golden jewels. Its icy blue eyes glistened inside the pyramid. At the foot of the statue sat the Siamese cat. Its body was turned from Jenna, its head bowed in submission.

She looked around and saw several stone carvings, roughly the same height as her, dispersed around the pyramid. Atop of each one, was an amber globe emitting soft orange light. She walked towards one and stood in front of it. *It's a mummy! They're all mummies!* Her eyes gazed into the globe, deep into its sun-fire centre. Inside was a sea of moving light. It was tranquil, like a gentle wave. Jenna marvelled at the dance of colour, while patiently waiting for some form of instruction.

A faint voice soon appeared, breaking the silence.

Jenna looked over only to find that the Siamese cat had left. "Where are you?"

"I am everywhere. I *surround* you."

Jenna's sense of adventure was starting to wane. She'd been fearless up until now. But she couldn't shake the nagging suspicion that the pyramid was all part of a trap.

"Look into its eyes, and you will see the truth."

"What truth? What will I see?"

There was no answer. Her eyes slowly travelled up the body of the colossal statue. Upon reaching its electric blue stare, she froze. Within seconds, her mind was pulled into another world.

The eyes were telling Jenna a story; one that was faintly reminiscent of her grandmother's tale. She saw nine cats surrounding a city—the city of Menao. It was as if she was there in person, standing next to them. Silently, she observed, as four strangers approached. They knelt before one of the cats and cast their arms into the air, cursing the stars.

Jenna remembered the story: they had come for the talisman.

The animal fought for its freedom, but was captured and removed from its position of authority. The men covered its body in a thick, brown sack. Then, without any cares for their theft, they stole the animal from its home.

Jenna watched as King Odon's servants chanted around the base of his statue. The remaining cats then turned into stone. Each was wrapped with its ruby medallion in protective cloth. The servants then bowed to King Odon. They left quietly and discreetly as they began their voyage of secrecy.

With a heavy heart, Jenna witnessed the demise of the city as it fell into ruins. People screamed as the ground broke all around them. Lightning torched the sky. Walls shattered. Buildings collapsed. Everything was swallowed into an abyss. Destruction conquered their civilization, Menao was now gone.

Suddenly, Jenna was whisked back to the pyramid, to where she was standing. An ill feeling of doom hijacked her thoughts. Quickly, she ran over to the entrance. She wanted out. Staring at the wall, she was shocked to see that the opening had vanished. There were no seams or lines, nothing visible whatsoever.

Jenna spun around when the voice she'd heard earlier, returned. Standing behind her now, was an old woman.

"Hello, there." The woman's body was frail, yet strong; her voice soft, but firm.

"Grandma—is that you?"

"Yes . . ."

"I don't understand—what's going on?"

Her tone was delicately deceiving. "You are the keeper of the key, Jenna. And we need your help." Her appearance was pleasantly spiritual but also slightly worrisome. Jenna had never been afraid of her grandmother before, but right now she couldn't tell whether she was speaking as a kindly apparition or a diabolic phantom.

"What key? What are you talking about?" Jenna's stance was mobile. She was ready to run at any given moment.

"This is the Temple of Esemais," her grandmother said. "This is King Odon's temple, and my home. I've brought you here to see Menao." Slowly, she began to move towards Jenna.

With her back up against the wall, Jenna looked for a way out. "This is just an illusion—I'm not really here."

"This is our Kingdom," she continued. "You are here to see the truth. It lies within this temple."

Jenna just shook her head.

"And that," her grandmother pointed behind her, "is King Odon. He is King of the Cats. He has guarded this temple since the beginning of our time."

"But I followed the Siamese cat, so, this must be a dream!"

"No—no dream. The cat is real, you must trust it."

Jenna took a step sideways.

Her grandmother stopped, abruptly. "Do not fear us, Jenna. Not yet . . ." With that, she turned and drifted back to his statue.

"Wait—what do you mean 'us'?"

"You will soon find out . . ." The words flowed behind her.

Jenna knew that something was making her grandmother act this way; such bizarre behaviour was not hers alone. She seemed possessed.

"Remember, it thrives on darkness. The light will help you." She pointed to the door where the opening reappeared. "You must leave now. Leave before they waken." Her body then disappeared behind the statue.

"Before *who* wakens?" Jenna yelled. "I don't understand!"

The silence that followed was soon drowned out by an unearthly crash. Jenna screamed when a thundering bolt of white-hot lightning broke through the pinnacle of the pyramid, reaching the ground around her. With one giant fork of electricity, each statue buzzed and beamed. Jenna cupped her ears to muffle the horrifying sounds.

Each amber globe turned a grizzly shade of red and then lifted into the air. One by one, they exploded as pieces of glass were propelled in all directions. Jenna quickly covered her head and crouched down on the quaking ground to avoid the spatter of broken glass. Shards lay all around her, quivering to the beats of the moving earth. "What's happening?" she shrieked.

Her eyes scanned the walls for the opening. As she searched, she felt something trickle down the side of her face. A small, crimson droplet fell onto a piece of glass by her feet. She dipped her finger into the substance and sniffed it. "Oh no!" Gently, she touched the skin above her left eye. Lowering her hand, she saw that her fingers were drizzled in blood. A thin ribbon of red now flowed from a wound. "Oh my God!"

She was momentarily distracted by something that moved behind her. Turning back, she saw the stone statues coming to life. One after the other, they broke through their moulds. With fervor, they dragged their heavy bodies through the glass as they stretched out their arms to grab her.

"Get away from me!" Jenna cried. She lashed out her legs to stop them. "I've got to get out of here!" With one hand pressed against her head, she ran for the opening.

The mummies sped up to chase her as she fled.

Jenna burst through the entrance. The cool night air brought relief to her immediately. She paused to look back. The pyramid was gone. All that was left was the moon, the stars and the white desert sand.

"How do I get out of this nightmare?" she scowled.

A swirling mass of tightly tucked winds suddenly blew past her, answering her question. It knocked her onto the ground giving her little time to react. She lifted herself up with her fingers but felt the ground tremble, just as it did inside the pyramid. But the ground wasn't shaking, it was sinking. And something was pulling her under.

Her mouth opened to scream but nothing came out. Seconds later, she relaxed. The pain from her head faded and the bleeding stopped. A silky glaze coated her eyes, leaving them open in a strange hypnotic stare. Captured in the moment, her body fell into a deep trance.

There, she remained safely out of harm's way, where her worries could no longer find her.

DREAM, NIGHTMARE, OR SOMETHING ELSE

"It's okay—I think she's back," a familiar voice spoke.

"Jenna . . . Jenna . . ." another chimed in.

Jenna's body remained in place as the girdle of space around her, rotated. Faster and faster it spun as images before her coalesced into a churning gray cloud. She felt like a leaf inside a tornado, within the eye of the storm, somehow guarded by the winds.

Up ahead, was a gleaming, yellow light. It stood out amongst the gray as it floated on the air towards her. Jenna's arms extended outward; she wanted to touch it. A fixed point amongst the turbulent orbit of air, she reached and reached for it. She could see it moving closer—a small, shiny, chiselled instrument.

The air was spinning . . . spinning . . . spinning. Then, with a sudden blink—

"Oh good, you're back," her mother said, from across the kitchen table. "You were starting to tell us about a trip you went on last night. A dream about the desert . . ." she smiled.

For a moment, Jenna just stared. Her eyes then combed the room for abnormalities but nothing was out of place.

A cold chill embraced the top-left side of her face as something warm sat by the ridge of her mouth. Still, she didn't move.

Her mother waited for a response, while sipping a cup of tea.

"What were you going to tell us?" Jenna's grandmother said, from the other side of the table. "You drifted off, dear."

"I did?" Jenna glanced down and saw her right hand curled around a silver spoon. It sat next to her lips, heaping with vegetable soup. A little cloud of steam escaped into the air; the soup was hot. Inside her other hand was a cold, folded cloth, which now pressed against her forehead.

She placed the spoon on the table and lifted the cloth from her head. Her fingers brushed over a small, swollen knob. "Ouch . . ."

"You took a nasty fall last night and bumped your head. It's just a little goose egg," her grandmother said. "How do you feel, now?"

Jenna cringed as she touched it. "It hurts, but I'm okay, don't worry. It's not the worse thing I've done to myself."

Her mother stood from the table. "Well, as long as you're okay, sweetie. That's the important thing. Keep the cold compress on it. Grandma will take care of you. I've got to get back to your father, he's still working in the clinic."

"Okay," Jenna said. Her confusion began to clear when she remembered the sick animals.

"And next time, tie your shoelaces!" she teased. "We don't want any more accidents with you tripping over your sneakers." She opened the door and headed outside.

"I tripped over my shoelaces—that's how I hurt my head?" Jenna highly doubted that story.

"You seemed to be running from something," her grandmother said. "What was it that you were running from?"

"I don't know. But I had the weirdest dream last night . . ."

"Well, you're here now," she said. "Oh goodness, will you look at the time. I've got errands to run. Keep that cloth on your head, at least until the bump goes down. I'll be back. I won't be long, I promise."

Eyes like a hawk, Jenna watched as her grandmother exited the room.

Her mind played over the events of the previous night. She hadn't forgotten a single detail, not even the touch of her own blood.

She decided not to think about it anymore. The entire scenario was crazy and improbable; all it was doing was tangling her thoughts. Jenna came to the conclusion that none of her experience made any sense, except for the part about the lost city. Even then, she was grasping at straws.

She left the kitchen and headed for her room. A feeling of comfort washed over her when she saw Ted and Tony stretched out on her bed. Lying on their sides, they looked like two lop-sided balloons. Neither of them woke when she entered the room. She was surprised however, to see something red and shiny dangling from her window.

Looking at it, she squinted. "What is that?"

Her feet trudged across the floor as she attempted to identify the new object. Placing her hand beneath it, she twirled it with the tips of her fingers. "It's a star—"

A small, red crystal sprinkled the light from outside onto the walls of the room. The cats awoke with laggard yawns, but at first sight of the red shadow, they jumped into hunt mode and began their pursuit of the pseudo-prey.

"I bet Grandma put this here, but why? Why didn't she say anything about it?" Jenna deliberated the star's meaning and whether it had any connection to her dream.

Regardless of her inexplicable experience, the city was overwhelmed with mystery. Animals were getting sick and people were disappearing. Jenna couldn't ignore the facts. And the more she thought about it, the more she realized just how much her family was involved. Her mother was the curator of the museum where the strange mummy had arrived, and her father was the vet who had first discovered the sick animals.

Like a magnet, these problems seemed to be attracted to her family. Soon, Jenna figured, they would be knocking at her front door.

EVER SO WATCHFUL

Jenna now sat at the kitchen table twirling her fingers. Silently, she watched her grandmother unload grocery bags. She wanted to believe that the stories she'd been told were fiction, but after seeing the star hanging in her window, she wanted answers.

She stood up from the chair and removed an icepack from the freezer. Keeping one eye on her grandmother, she wrapped a cloth around the pack. Placing it on her head, she grimaced. The bump was still tender.

Jenna moved closer to the sink, next to where her grandmother was standing.

The line between fiction and non-fiction was crumbling, leaving her confused about what was fact and what was fable. She needed to hear the real story, in her kitchen, at that moment. She was tired of thinking that she was losing her marbles.

"What is your question, Jenna?" her grandmother said.

"Grandma, please tell me what's going on. I feel like I'm losing my grip on reality. The things I've seen these last few days have been somewhat of a torment. Has it all been just a dream? I mean . . . where were you last night?"

She took a moment to consider the question. "Some things cannot be explained. Your parents are extremely busy right now, and so I must protect you." Her eyes were focused on the sink. "I know that you saw me last night."

Jenna caught a glimpse of her grandmother's reflection in the window. Her face was distorted. In the glass she saw the outline of a furry, black mouth with long, white fangs hanging down.

Jenna shook her head and looked again, but the image was gone. "What's happening to you?"

Her grandmother let out a desperate sigh. "I'm changing, Jenna."

"Oh, I get it. This is another one of my dreams, isn't it?"

"No, it isn't. You need to believe."

"Believe *what*? What does that mean?"

"Search your mind for the answers and your heart for the truth," she said. "Use the key to unlock the door. There, you will find what you are looking for. Give me your hand, for the path begins here."

Jenna decided to play along. As she opened her hand, her grandmother placed a small golden key into her palm. She then wrapped her fingers around it. "It is now your destiny to help us. And you must hurry—we're running out of time."

She turned on the taps as the sink began to fill with water. Each droplet sounded heavy, leaden. What started as a trickle soon turned into a typhoon; a cyclone of—

Jenna coughed herself awake. Her upper body was slumped over the kitchen table and her forehead was swimming in a puddle of cool water. She raised her head and saw that the ice pack had melted on the table.

A soft bark came from the floor, helping her to regain consciousness. Looking down, she saw the sweet eyes of her black Labrador. "Sammy, what is it boy?" She leaned over and stroked his back. "You want out, don't you?"

Playfully, he scampered out the door as Jenna held it open. He then turned and inspected something by her feet. Bending down, she noticed a small black box sitting by the door with a white envelope leaning against it. She brought both items into the house and set them on the kitchen table. She opened the envelope and removed a thin, red piece of parchment with black lettering neatly stencilled on it.

'For Jenna,' the paper read. '*You are very wise to be careful and very careful to be wise. Consider these four thoughts like the sides of the pyramid: 1—You must find the door; 2—Look for what is behind it; 3—Use the key to unlock what is locked; 4—Take what you need with you.*'

Jenna paused to let the words sink in.

'*Know this: your heart is the secret, and the secret is the path to closure. Only then will there be peace. You must understand that time has been taken. It must be returned!*'

Now, more than ever, Jenna wanted answers. She opened the box and out fell a sparkly blue, pocket-sized pyramid. She picked it up and held it in her hand.

"That's pretty," her grandmother said, entering the room. "How's your head? Feeling any better?"

"No, I think I might have to get it checked, actually," she laughed.

"Would you like some tea? I'm making some."

"No, thanks." Her eyes were fastened to the object resting in her palm.

"Oh, by the way, I found this in your room." She removed something from her pocket and placed it on the table. I believe you dropped it," she said, leaving the kitchen.

The last thing Jenna saw was her grandmother's evasive grin.

With a golden key resting on the table in front of her, Jenna now knew that some of the story had meaning. And, that somewhere out there, were the answers she longed for.

All she had to do was find them.

RETURN TO THE MUMMY

In Jenna's mind, it was clear: the skeleton in the backyard belonged to a cat—*the* cat. There was no denying what she saw. All she had to do was envision the bones with skin and fur. She believed that the skeleton and the Siamese cat were one of the same, like two sides of a coin. The cat she followed into the cornfield was the same one she saw when she walked home from the museum. But with all the encounters she'd had with it, it didn't try to harm her. Jenna couldn't understand then, why all the neighbourhood pets were getting so violently ill.

She paced back and forth over the bedroom carpet while her eyes centered on the red crystal hanging from the window. *Is the Siamese cat purposely going after animals, or are they just getting in the way of it?*

Jenna looked down at her watch; it was almost four o'clock in the afternoon. In a few hours it would be getting dark. After some careful thinking, she devised a plan.

Wasting little time, she changed into her most comfortable jeans and purple shirt that had, *'Cats are for real. People are for show!'* printed on it. Feeling her forehead, she smiled; the lump had almost disappeared.

She placed a sweater inside the backpack along with a flashlight, a pen, some paper and a Polaroid camera. She stuck the golden key inside her pocket and then raced down the stairs with the bag in tow.

There was one last thing she wanted to do before leaving the house. She opened the back door and hustled over to the skeleton. The picnic blanket was tossed to one side. She picked it up and stared at it. The middle part had been completely shredded, as if something had torn its way through. "Oh yeah, I'm definitely getting my head checked after this."

The bones lay undisturbed in the ground. Jenna took out the camera and snapped a few pictures of the skeleton. Moments later, they came into view, each one nice and clear. The ivory bones were striking against the dark earth. When she was done, she placed the blanket over the hole and set the rocks back onto the corners to test her theory.

Things were quiet—eerily quiet.

When her task was completed, she returned to the house to gather some food. She found some granola bars, stuffed them into the backpack and then quickly scribbled a note to her family, letting them know that she would be spending the night at her friend, Tamara's house.

After hugging the pets, she headed for the front door.

Jenna knew that she had to go back to the museum. It was all starting to make sense. The Siamese Mummy was the key.

* * *

When she entered the front doors of the Lionhead Museum, a woman rose up to greet her. "Hello, Jenna. How are you?" It was Sheila Smith, another museum employee that Jenna had come to know quite well. She was also Jason's mother.

"I'm okay, keeping busy."

Sheila was a well-dressed, sprightly woman, with the perkiest blonde hair that Jenna had ever encountered. Today however, she looked as though she had lost some of her spunk.

"How's Jason doing?" Jenna asked. "Has he been playing baseball without me?"

Sheila's stance changed instantly to reflect a woman now burdened with woes. Her voice became grim at the mere mention of her son. "Jason hasn't been playing baseball at all, not since he got sick."

"But I just saw him a few days ago. What happened?"

"He was bitten by a neighbour's dog. The doctors think that he's been infected with rabies. They're still doing tests."

Jenna gasped. "*What?* Is he okay?"

"Well, he's better than he was a few days ago," she said, rubbing her eyes. "I've been at the hospital for the last few days but everyone there told me to take a break. So I came here."

"That's awful, I'm so sorry. Can I go see him?"

"Actually, you can't. The doctors aren't allowing anyone near him except his family."

"Oh." Jenna's tone was sedate. Jason was one of her closest companions in Wichita. He was the first person to befriend her both at school and on the baseball field. "Will you let me know when I can visit him?"

She nodded, "Of course."

Jenna thought about the attack. "Whose dog was it?"

"It was Tommy's dog, Biscuit. He was crazed, and his aggression was completely unprovoked."

Jenna said nothing, she was utterly speechless.

Sheila glanced around the lobby. "Have you heard about all the disappearances? I can't believe it. They said that eighty people have gone missing now, and no one knows where they are. The police still don't know anything. And it seems random—people disappearing from all over Wichita. All ages and no connection."

"*Eighty* people?" Jenna's voice staggered. "That's so many!"

"It's just terrible, isn't it? Listen, I better go. I've got some things to do here and then I'm heading back to the hospital."

"Of course . . . I understand," she smiled. "Please give my best to Jason." She began to walk away but then stopped. "Oh wait, I forgot to ask—do you know where Anna is today?"

Sheila shrugged. "I don't know. She was supposed to come in this morning but didn't show up. We're still trying to get a hold of her."

"I hope everything's okay—she probably just forgot that she was working today." Jenna looked off towards the escalator. "And do you know who's working in the Egyptian room?"

"Kenneth was here earlier but left for a break just after three. He hasn't come back yet."

"Oh, okay, thank you." Seeing the sadness in Sheila's eyes, Jenna walked over and hugged her. "Take care."

"You too, sweetie."

The two women parted and went their separate ways.

Jenna wondered about Anna as she stepped onto the escalator. She hoped that nothing was wrong. *And poor Jason*, she thought. *My best friend!* She knew that Biscuit must have infected him the same night that he tried to attack her. But something had stopped him. Jenna knew she was lucky.

Although it was difficult, she had to set aside her thoughts of Jason and focus on what she came for.

As her feet rested on the second floor, she remembered that her grandmother had gone to visit the Thailand exhibit first on the day they came to see the mummy. So, she decided to retrace her steps.

She made a left turn in front of the Egyptian wing and headed down the hall towards the section that said, *'TOUR OF ASIA'. What was it that Grandma needed to see in there?* she wondered.

Entering the first room, she looked around carefully. On the left was the Mongolian exhibit and on the right was the history of Korea and China. She continued on. This section of the museum was quite large, as she passed many countries before she found the Thailand exhibit. Then she saw a banner ahead of her, '*Welcome to the Land of Siam*'. Below, was an enormous poster of a Siamese cat.

Jenna was confused. "Why is the Siamese Mummy in the Egyptian wing? What else would Grandma come to see in this room?"

She knew that the Siamese cat was from Thailand, not Egypt, and that the sapphire temple she'd been taken to, was also in Thailand. She thought for a moment. "The thieves must have taken the cat to Egypt."

It was now time to return to the Siamese Mummy.

Jenna was headed for the Egyptian wing when she heard voices behind her. Looking back, she saw no one. Her attention was then drawn to a room down the hall where a heavy thud came from inside. She ran towards the sound and saw an old man lying on the floor in front of the Siamese Mummy.

She rushed over to help him. "Are you okay?"

The old man looked up at her and squinted. "Is that you, Mary?"

"No, my name is Jenna. Are you hurt?"

He took a deep breath and sat up. "No, I'm all right. I don't know what happened. I was looking at that mummy and I think I fainted."

Jenna helped him up. "Is there someone here with you? Someone I can call for?"

He shook his head. "I came alone."

She put her arm around the old man and walked him over to the bench by the wall. "Did you touch the case at all?"

"No, I don't think so. Wait . . . actually yes, yes I did. I was trying to read the print inside the case and I couldn't see without my glasses. I fumbled trying to find them but never did. So, I leaned in and read it." In an instant, his manner changed. "I feel fine now." He lifted his head up. "Sorry to have worried you. Thank you for your help, though, you're very kind."

Jenna smiled. "Would you like me to help you downstairs?"

"No, thank you," he said, standing quickly. He pushed her aside and shuffled out of the room.

Okay, that was odd, she thought. Jenna surveyed the area where the man had fallen. A pair of glasses now lay on the floor. She ran over, picked them up and darted after him. She came to a stop at the top of the escalator. "Hello—" she called out. The man was nowhere in sight.

Looking down, she noticed a thin, ragged scrap of clothing by her feet. It was a piece of fabric from the man's shirt. Jenna recognized it at once. "Hello—" she tried again.

The man had touched the display case and was now gone. A cold shiver bullied up her spine. Something was very wrong. She wondered why the security feature surrounding the mummy hadn't been activated. Her grandmother had warned her about an alarm that would go off if anyone touched the glass case. *Why would she say something like that if it wasn't true?*

Nevertheless, Jenna had identified the source of the problem. And in her heart she knew, it was waiting for her in the very next room.

SPELLBOUND

Jenna stared at the Siamese Mummy for quite some time. Like before, she was mesmerized by its presence and could feel strength beaming from its tightly woven body. She felt overwhelmed by its power and was once again compelled to touch it.

No, Jenna, she scolded herself. *Something bad might happen.* She made a mental note of the old man who disappeared. *I think Grandma's right—the Siamese Mummy is cursed!* Her gut feeling confirmed it.

The hairs on the back of her neck began to rise. All thoughts were on this animal. *What is it doing right now?* she wondered. Her brain demanded information; she wanted to know everything about it. Visually, she dissected every part of the display.

She noticed something that she hadn't before. An old, browned, tattered document sat propped up next to the animal. A drawing of a star surrounded by red and white flowers was painted on it. Swiftly, she sifted through her memories. It reminded her of something that she'd seen before. With careful precision, she read the inscription below the drawing.

'*The Star of Omandai was a sacred ruby which many believed, belonged to this mummy. Its purpose is unknown, although it is speculated that in life, the ruby was worn around the animal's neck. The Star has never been found. All that is left is this drawing.*'

So far, the words supported her grandmother's story. Jenna continued reading.

'*This specimen was unearthed in 1909 in Luxor, Egypt, near the Valley of the Kings. The two archeologists who discovered it both disappeared shortly after, and were never found. In their journals they stated that the mummy was a sacrificial offering to appease the gods of Siam for having one of their royal cats die in Egypt. It was buried near the Valley of the Kings to signify its position of power. It was kept hidden from public view until now.*'

"Wow, that's amazing . . ." Jenna boasted. Still, she couldn't help but wonder why she was being pulled into the story. As she considered the reasons, her fingers began to fiddle with the key in her pocket. And then something clicked in her mind. "The key!"

Jenna knew that the back rooms of the museum were filled with artefacts and fossils, anything ancient. Most of the work was done behind closed doors. Fossils were prepared, museum pieces were catalogued and research was conducted. Most of the artefacts were kept in storage rooms and only a small percentage of museum pieces were on display for the public.

Jenna had a feeling that the key was meant to open something in one of the back rooms. She remembered the access code for the door behind the Egyptian wing; she had watched her mother enter it many times.

Stepping out into the hallway, she then turned down a narrow corridor. Quiet and sneaky, she dashed to the other end until she came upon a thin, square, silver keypad by the door. Promptly, she entered the numbers. The door made a low buzzing sound and then opened. Jenna slipped through the doorway and watched as it closed behind her.

Searching the room, she discovered that she was alone. The space was filled to the brim with pieces. Everywhere she turned, ancient artefacts surrounded her. The gray, metal shelving units spanned from the floor to the ceiling and consisted of open concept. You could see straight through them. Each unit was roughly thirty feet long, stretching almost the entire length of the room. There was one for each aisle and Jenna counted nine aisles. She had a lot of exploring to do.

Without hesitating, she began her hunt.

* * *

Each aisle seemed to take forever. She travelled up and down, looking at all the items that were present. Bowls, vases, statues, jewellery—so far, nothing required a key.

After an hour of scrutinizing labour, she stopped. A rattling noise came from inside the vase she was holding. "This is beautiful." The object was deep cardinal red, encrusted with black and silver jewels. With her hand inside the vessel, she sighed. A small glass marble was the culprit. She withdrew her arm, placed the vase back in position and continued on down the aisle.

Her investigation was cut short when the door to the room opened. Abruptly, she turned and snuck out of sight.

As silent as possible, she stood behind one of the metal stacks, peeking through to see who had entered. Her concentration was intense. She was well aware that she wasn't supposed to be in the room.

A man, whom Jenna had never seen before, walked into the room. He wore a gray-collared shirt with a black tie. His dark slacks accented his sable-coloured hair. An attractive man, Jenna thought, but with a murky aura around him.

He looked around and then advanced towards one of the shelves. He had the same suspicious frame that Jenna had—shifty and uncertain. He lifted up a large vase and reached inside of it. A small box was revealed when he removed his hand. He returned the vase, walked to the other side of the room and sat down.

With vigilant discretion, she observed his every move.

Carefully, he turned the box around in his hand. It was tiny and black, with gold-rippled edges. A shiny sheen slid over the surface as he angled it under the light.

Placing it down, he picked up the telephone on the table and dialled a number. "Yeah, it's me. I've got it here now," he said. His fingers strummed along the table as he spoke. "No, no one saw me. There's just one thing I need. Well, it's locked. No, I can't do that without destroying it. I'll leave it here, no one will find it. I can't take it out while people are here—it's too risky. I'll come back for it tonight when the museum is closed." He cleared his throat a few times and then continued. "Well, the rest must still be buried. I know they're worth a fortune! Okay, I've got to go." He then hung up.

Jenna mentally reviewed the conversation. *The man has a box which seems to be valuable. Why is he hiding it? And why is he being so secretive?* She had never seen this man before, and was beginning to think that he wasn't supposed to be in the back room. But who was she to judge.

One thing she did know, was that she didn't like him. He had a crooked manner; his behaviour seemed deviant. It took Jenna all of five minutes to sum him up and she didn't like what she saw. She was relatively good at reading people. This one was easy: the man was bad news.

When she put her hand on the shelf to steady herself, it moved. A small wooden bowl sitting near the edge, tipped back and forth, precariously. Her hands frantically grasped at the object as it disengaged from the shelf, but it was just out of her range. She cringed as it fell to the ground. The sound reverberated throughout the room. Looking back at the man, Jenna was startled to see that he was already on his way over to check out the noise.

Immediately, she ducked.

With a stern voice, he shouted, "Who's there?"

Jenna crouched down and moved a few aisles over. She repositioned her backpack and then paused to listen.

The man stopped and inspected the shelf. He waited a moment and then yelled again. "Who's there?"

Keeping low, Jenna peeked through the shelf.

As the man bent down to ponder the fallen bowl, the telephone rang. "This whole bloody place is cursed!" He stood and ran down the aisle. "Hello? No, Mr. Harrison is not available. I'm afraid you'll have to call back later."

He hung up the telephone and stood for a moment. Jenna assumed that he had forgotten about the bowl. Instead, he picked up the box and shifted it in his hands; he seemed hypnotized by it. After a few minutes of eye-locking magnetism, the man turned and walked over to one of the shelves. With a face full of distrust, he glanced around the room and then placed the box into a large vase.

Jenna awaited his next move. Happily, she watched as the man headed for the door. He took one more look around and then left.

For a few minutes she remained hidden, in case the man came back. After feeling it was safe, she stepped out towards the aisle. She decided that her next move would be to find the man's vase.

When she reached the intended aisle, she frowned. There were roughly forty different vases in all shapes and sizes on the shelf. She looked inside the first few but found nothing. Moving on, she continued searching.

Her one hand was inside a black, gold-laced vase when suddenly the door re-opened. Panic took over when she heard footsteps heading her way. *Oh no!*

The man had returned.

With nimble steps, Jenna moved out of site as she tried to control her breathing.

The man rushed back to the aisle where he'd stashed the box.

Jenna immediately looked inside the vase she was holding, praying to the gods that she didn't have the one he wanted. Her body relaxed when she saw that it was empty. *What is he doing?* she wondered.

Once again, he picked up the vase and peered inside of it. He then placed it back, scouted the area and exited the room.

Wow—talk about paranoid! Jenna snickered to herself. She waited behind the shelf until the coast was clear, and then walked back to the aisle. This time she knew exactly which vase the box was in; there was no need for guessing.

Placing her hands carefully on each side, she lifted the artefact off of the shelf and lowered it onto the floor. She reached inside and felt a cold, square object sitting at the bottom. A smile enveloped her face when she lifted it out of the vase. It was the box.

She held it beneath the ceiling light and rotated it with her fingers. On the front was a keyhole. "The key! The key! Of course!" Jenna reached into her pocket and extracted the golden key that her grandmother had given her. She placed it inside the hole and with a tiny turn, the box lid opened.

A faint whisper escaped the trinket. Jenna listened attentively to the sound. Then, with miniscule movements, she opened the lid all the way. Her fingers touched the sides of something hard, polished and broken. She removed the object and gasped. "Oh wow!" She recognized it from the drawing inside the mummy's case. It was the Star of Omandai, but only half of it. "Where's the other part?" Imagining the pieces together, Jenna estimated the size to be that of a small plum.

She placed the ruby on the table and examined the box. Flipping it over, she saw something etched on the bottom. It looked like letters. 'SITSABUB'. "What on Earth?" Then, she read the letters backwards. 'BUBASTIS'. Her brain registered the word. Jenna knew what the letters spelled and furthermore, she knew exactly what to do next.

In haste, she removed the sweater from her backpack. She sat the ruby back inside the box, wrapped it in the sweater and shoved everything into the bag. In her mind it was perfectly clear: the box was coming with her.

She returned the vase to the shelf and quickly exited the room.

Heading back to the Siamese Mummy, Jenna understood that her mission had been expedited. For her, it wasn't a problem. Besides, she was a 'fly by the seat of her pants' kind of girl. She learned on the move.

Upon entering the room, Jenna heard a whisper. Slowly, she approached the mummy. Cries now came from inside the case, from within its glass tomb. A mournful lament of pain and sorrow. Muffled growls. Stifled roars. It was calling to her.

And this time, Jenna was listening.

DR. OSIRIS

Jenna was surprised that the sun had disappeared, considering the forecast for the day had showed no rain. But the last few days had brought an array of unexpected weather. Chaotic winds and beautiful sunshine; lightning storms and beautiful sunshine; rain showers and beautiful sunshine. Like an unsupervised seesaw, the conditions oscillated from one extreme to the other.

The sun had now drowned in a sea of black clouds. Once again, the weather was teetering.

Jenna didn't particularly care, though. Her mind was preoccupied with other matters. The Siamese Mummy, to be exact. She had left the museum fifteen minutes earlier and was now heading somewhere else by foot.

The soles of her shoes collided triumphantly with the pavement as she paraded down the street. She was on the road to solving a mystery. And that road was leading her right towards Dr. Osiris's house.

She held her backpack close to her body as the rain began to fall. It started off nice and mellow, as a warm July drizzle. But it soon turned into a relentless downpour, heavy on her skin. Through the veil of water, Jenna saw Dr. Osiris's house. Although it was only a block away, the distance was quite long. She had to get moving.

Her feet splashed through the water as she began to run past the houses. Peering through scrunched up eyes, she saw that her destination was near.

She breezed over the front lawn and quickly climbed the stairs of the rickety porch. Knocking on the door, she leaned over to catch her breath.

An old man's voice soon appeared. "Yes, yes, who's there?"

"Hello, Dr. Osiris—it's me," Jenna said. Her words dawdled as she inhaled big gulps of air.

A silver-haired man in his seventies, wearing a pair of brown, tweed pants and a cream-coloured cardigan, opened the door. "Well, hello, Jenna. What in heaven's name are you doing out in the rain? Come in, dear, come in."

She stepped inside and smiled back at the old man. "It sure is wet out there."

Acknowledging her state of dampness, he disappeared into the hallway bathroom and returned with two large towels. "Here—dry yourself off. And while you're doing that, I'll go get you a cup of hot chocolate. That should warm you up. Then, you can tell me what brought you out here today."

With a slight hunch in his step, he headed for the kitchen.

Dr. Osiris's house was only a twenty-minute walk from the museum, and about the same distance from Jenna's farm. It wasn't too long of a trek to get there. Right now, it was imperative that she talked to him.

She wiped herself dry with one of the towels and squeezed the moisture out of her hair with the other. Bending down, she opened her backpack. With one look, her eyes swept through the hallway. Seeing no one, she unfolded the sweater inside the backpack and placed the black box at the bottom. Under no circumstances was Jenna going to tell anyone about what she found or took from the museum. The only person she wanted to report to was her mother, but now was not the time. She removed the sweater from the bag and put it on. The fabric warmed her immediately.

Her intuition told her that the man inside the museum was not supposed to have the box, and that he might have, in fact, stolen it. Jenna also knew that although the ruby was considered a valuable treasure, its worth was much more than just monetary.

She closed the backpack and waited for Dr. Osiris to return. Her mind recalled all the amazing things he had collected throughout the years. His home was filled with ancient artefacts and antiques. This was to be expected since Dr. Osiris had been an archaeology professor for many years, as well as curator of the Lionhead Museum. This of course, was before he left his career behind to become a member of the farming community.

His colleagues had thought that the switch was nonsensical, especially for a man of his age. Dr. Osiris was adamant however, in proving that he was of sound mind, and that farm work could be just as gratifying. He simply wanted something different.

Jenna looked around the hallway and then wandered into the study. Lining the dark, wooden walls were shelves full of scientific magazines, periodicals and extravagantly-titled literary journals. Many of the titles were difficult for her to understand since most of them were printed in foreign text.

Jenna had visited Dr. Osiris many times over the past year and had sat for countless hours discussing ancient civilizations and cultures with him. He was a fascinating man, with many stories to tell. He was the male equivalent of her grandmother.

As an undergraduate student, he researched the life of King Khafre—a pharaoh who built one of the pyramids of Giza, and who was also credited for building the Great Sphinx.

For his master's degree, Dr. Osiris travelled to Egypt, to the eastern shore of the Nile. He was on an expedition in Thebes to study the resting place of Inyotef I.

His true passion however, was discovered when he was conducting research for his doctorate. While in Egypt, he voyaged to a place just north of Cairo, called Bubastis. It was a site of worship for the cat goddess, Bastet. She was known as the patroness of music, dance and protector of pregnant women. It was also believed that she protected men from demons and disease.

Dr. Osiris and his team had found a burial chamber containing the remains of several hundred mummified cats. It was the peak of his career because there, he had found his calling. He spoke about that time in his life quite often. Jenna knew that if he was given the chance to go back and relive it, he would.

He later took a job at the Wichita State University teaching African history. Although he enjoyed teaching, he found his time better spent in museums, where he could be in direct contact with the artefacts, especially the dead ones. At first, he was cross-appointed with the Lionhead Museum, but eventually he gave up his teaching career and accepted the title of curator for the museum.

A little over a year ago, Dr. Osiris retired from the museum. He began a business in farming, alongside his two sons, Michael and Peter. His neighbours thought it was strange that he didn't have a farm of his own. Regardless of that fact, he was busy in his new position. On Jenna's street alone, he was managing three crops. And he was doing an exceptional job; all the landowners were happy.

Together, the three men had gained a reputable name. The sons worked the fields while Dr. Osiris managed the finances and the people. Jenna often saw the men and their machines in her cornfield. She assumed that they were Dr. Osiris's sons since she had never met them in person.

Deep in thought, her mind was far from where she was standing. She practically jumped out of her skin when something tapped her on the shoulder. She spun around and saw the old man standing behind her with a mug full of steaming chocolate. "Dr. Osiris—you scared me."

He chuckled, handed her the drink and then sat down in the rocking chair by the window.

Jenna took a sip and gazed around the room. "I swear, this room gets bigger and bigger every time I visit."

"Sit down, Jenna, and tell me what brought you out here today."

"Well . . . I have a question about something, and I figured that you would have the answer. Do you know anything about this new cat mummy at the museum?" She tried to give Dr. Osiris the impression that she was unfamiliar with the topic.

He turned his head towards the window and released a heavy sigh. "Not a good day for farming, is it? Not a good day at all."

Jenna looked at him, curiously. He was acting like he hadn't heard her. His fingers now toyed with the gold ring he wore. It was a parting gift from the staff at the Lionhead museum: a thick gold band with the head of a male lion finely crafted on top of it. It was symbolic of both his study of cats and his years at the museum.

A loud, repetitive ringing suddenly distracted them both. "Jenna—I'll be right back," he said, leaving the room.

Like a shadow, she followed. Stepping into the hallway, she heard a door close. Dr. Osiris was speaking to someone on the telephone, in his office down the hall.

"What do you mean it's gone?" he said, raising his voice. "Who else was there? Well, it didn't just walk away. There must have been someone else. Think hard. You better find it—our future depends on that piece!"

Jenna heard the phone slam down, and then Dr. Osiris talking out loud. *Who's he talking to?* she wondered. *Is someone else here?*

Then, another voice began to speak.

It's probably just Michael or Peter, she reasoned. Quietly, she tiptoed back into the study. She perused one of the shelves for something to read. Removing a journal, she flipped through the pages but all of the words were in Arabic.

Placing it back, her eyes glanced to the other side of the room. An impressively large, black, hardcover book with the title, *A City Lost,* was sitting on top of a short, wooden table in the corner.

Jenna walked over to the book. She opened the cover and thumbed through the pages. There were no pictures, only text. The book seemed to be telling a story. She read one of the pages and stopped when she saw the words 'King Odon'.

When she lifted the book to take a closer look, a pile of papers fell out onto the floor. She returned the book and bent down to pick the papers up. Jenna was surprised to see that each one was a map. *Cool—this is interesting.* One was so damaged, though, that when she touched it, it nearly disintegrated in her hands. "Oh, great."

She decided to just put everything back.

One of the sheets was lying upside down on the floor. Turning it over, she gulped. This map showed her parent's farm and two others on either side of it; three altogether. More specifically, it was a map of the cornfields. Two fields were circled with red and had large X's crossed through them. Hers did not. At the bottom of the map was a legend with soil and ground data.

Scribbled beneath each farm was a black box, a question mark and an arrow. *'The missing half?'* was written underneath each one.

Jenna was flabbergasted. This was Dr. Osiris's map. *Why would he be interested in what was underneath the cornfields?*

She stared intensely at the map. *Is this the missing half of the Star of Omandai? Is it under the cornfield? My cornfield?* And then it hit her: Dr. Osiris was looking for the ruby. *Oh my God—he knows!*

She thought back to all of her visits with him. Each time like clock-work, he would ask her about the cornfield. Different questions each time. Odd ones like, 'Do your pets go in the cornfield? Have you ever been lost in there? Do you know how to get out?' She didn't understand the meaning at the time. She just thought they were random questions; an old man making small talk.

Jenna now realized that Dr. Osiris was interested in the cornfields because of the land they were planted on. She looked down at the arrows pointing to the crops. She was hoping that her discovery was somehow a mistake, and that the map belonged to someone else. The benefit of the doubt however, was all washed away when she remembered Dr. Osiris's telephone conversation. Someone had called to report that something was missing. It was most likely the ruby—the one that she had taken.

Jenna wanted to reverse the last few minutes. She had inadvertently stumbled upon something that she didn't want to know.

In an attempt to return things to normal, she placed the papers back inside the book. The map of the farms slipped out as she closed the cover. "Oh, for Pete's sake!" She leaned over and picked it up. But before she had a chance to return it, a noise came from behind her.

Turning, she shrieked.

A tall, thin man stood in the room, watching her. "What are you doing?"

"I was . . . just . . . visiting," she said, hiding the map behind her back.

"This isn't your house, you shouldn't be snooping around!"

"You know what—you're absolutely right!" She smiled to alleviate the conflict. "In fact, I was just leaving . . ."

Dr. Osiris then ran into the room. "No, Peter—that's Jenna."

Peter said nothing, nor did he reach out his hand to greet her.

Dr. Osiris looked at him as if he were reprimanding a bad child. "It's *okay* for Jenna to look around."

The next thing he gave was an apology. "I'm sorry for Peter's rude behaviour. He's just a little stressed today. That said, he and I need to talk. We'll have to continue our visit another time."

Jenna agreed. "I have to go anyway. It was nice meeting you, Peter." She then hurried out of the room, picked up her backpack and ran out the front door. Her heart was pounding. Peter was completely cold towards her, not one part of him was amicable.

In the last few minutes, all Jenna wanted to do was get out of that house—a house that she once thought of as inviting.

She remained on the porch deliberating her next move. The sky was dark and the rain was still falling. Not the best day to be walking, but she had no other choice. Neither Dr. Osiris nor his son had offered to give her a ride home.

Gazing down, she realized that the map was still cupped in her hand. Although an accidental theft, Jenna was not going to return it. She had no intention of going back into that house.

Folding the paper, she placed it inside her pocket. She then dodged out into the street.

Her body ran at a steady pace in the direction of home. She felt herself dripping with water from head to toe. All of her clothes were saturated.

She slowed to a walk and took a few deep breaths. As her legs trudged through the wet street, something jingled inside of her head. Something was trying to get her attention. She stopped and looked around. Jenna had the distinct feeling that she was being followed. Searching the blackness, she saw nothing.

Looking back, she was startled by the headlights of a vehicle speeding towards her. Her entire body went numb. She just stood there, motionless in the heavy rain, wondering what to do next. The lights came closer, but still she didn't move. Her mind was stuck on the road, planted by the feet that refused to run.

Jenna braced for impact as the car screeched to a stop in front of her. Terrified, she screamed. The car sat on the road only a few feet from where she was standing.

Two doors flew open.

"Oh my God, Jenna!" her mother said, racing towards her. "You could have been hit!" She wrapped her arms around her and squeezed.

Her father ran up in front of her. "Jenna—are you okay?"

She didn't respond.

"Let's get her into the car," he said.

Together, they helped Jenna into the back seat. Her mother climbed in beside her. Taking her hand, she frowned. "Jenna—can you hear me?"

Her father jumped into the driver's seat and slammed the door. "She's probably in shock."

"Jenna? Are you okay?" her mother tried again.

"I'm . . . I'm . . . I'm sorry . . . Mom," she said, breaking her silence.

"Oh, thank God! You're okay!" she said, throwing a blanket over her shoulders. "Where have you been? We were worried sick about you. We called Tamara's house and you weren't there."

Her father turned the car around and accelerated down the street. "Let's get her home."

"I was . . . at . . . Dr. Osiris's house . . ." she started to explain. Suddenly, her body thrust forward and hit the passenger seat in front of her as the car came to an abrupt stop. She leaned back and felt her forehead. It was throbbing.

"Jesus! Is everyone okay back there?" her father shouted.

"Yes—I'm fine," her mother said. "Jenna?"

"I'm all right. My head hurts . . . but I'll be fine. What happened?"

Her father whispered, "Everyone be quiet—don't move!"

Jenna's internal alarm went off; she'd never heard her father talk like that before.

He sat now staring out the front window. His body was still and his eyes were focused straight ahead.

"Dad, what's going on?"

"Shhh . . ." he said.

"Reid—you're scaring us! What's happening?"

And then they all heard it; a low growl coming from the road ahead.

"Oh my god!" her mother shrieked.

Jenna's heart went crazy. Rain pelted the car from all sides which only made her pulse move faster. She looked out the front window and saw the Siamese cat poised in front of the car, preparing to jump on the hood. Its red eyes stood out amongst the darkness as it glared at the occupants. When it saw Jenna, it hesitated. Changing its posture, it slowly began to move around the car.

Jenna's father turned the key in the ignition but nothing happened. He slapped the dashboard angrily and then turned the key again. The car would not start. He lifted his head and saw the cat now walking alongside the driver's side.

It looked through the windows with an ill-tempered glare. Its jaws snapped over and over again, putting the fear of life into all three of them.

Jenna's father made another attempt to start the engine, when suddenly, the car came to life. The headlights beamed brightly on the wet road. He immediately put the car into 'reverse' and backed away. He then spun the wheel in the direction of the animal and drove the vehicle towards it, hoping to run it off the road.

It howled at the first sight of the headlights, and swung its big head away. It then leapt across the road, vanishing into a forest of trees beside them.

"Reid," Jenna's mother trembled, "what was that?"

"I don't know . . . but we need to get home right now! Hold on to something!"

NOT SAFE

Something sprinted across the backyard just as the car pulled up to the side of the house. With panic-stricken faces, Jenna and her parents ran for the back porch stairs. Jenna's father hollered for the dogs to come in.

They all stood at the doorway waiting for the pets. Max and Sam galloped through the rain towards the house. Jenna's mother took them by the collars and led them into the family room.

"Charlie!" Jenna's father yelled. But there was no sign of him.

Suddenly, a deep, penetrating roar came from the far end of the backyard. And Jenna knew—the Siamese cat was here.

CLOSE ENCOUNTERS

enna reached for the flashlight inside her backpack and turned it on. She then jumped down the porch stairs and rushed towards the cornfield.

"Jenna—come back!" her father screamed. "NO!"

His words disappeared behind her as she ran through the grass.

Full of adrenalin, Jenna called out, "Charlie, where are you? Charlie! Come to me, boy!"

Up ahead, she saw the eyes of the cat, and with one look she knew that something bad was about to happen.

Jenna lifted the flashlight and pointed it at the cat's eyes. Through the pouring rain, she watched it jerk its head away. She remembered her grandmother's words, *'It thrives on darkness, the light will help you.'* As she approached, it backed away, and thrashed its head from side to side in an agitated manner.

Thoughts from all around were stimulating Jenna's senses; everything was hitting her at once. The cat's fondness for darkness, it's avoidance of light, the strange upheaval in weather whenever it appeared. The answer, was in its eyes. *Its eyes!*

Jenna forced the light upon the cat. "What have you done with Charlie?" she cried.

It clapped its jaws and retreated from her, then looked off towards the cornfield.

She pointed the flashlight in the direction of the field. Something was in there; the stalks were moving.

Seconds later, Charlie exploded out in front of them. He landed by Jenna's feet and barked viciously at the feline intruder.

A sudden blast from behind took them all by surprise. Jenna looked back at the house and saw her father running towards them with a rifle aimed at the sky.

She wrapped her arms around Charlie and pulled him close, accidentally dropping the flashlight in the process.

With the light no longer shining on it, the cat growled and crept towards them. It was fixated on Charlie. Its mouth opened in a fearsome display of dominance.

"No!" Jenna yelled. "Get away from us!" With a blunt kick she lashed out at the cat. It ducked back and then leapt forward towards Charlie.

Jenna jumped in front of him and lashed out again. The cat dropped low to the ground as her leg sailed over its head. Its body was robust, yet agile.

Then, with one blow of its heavy paw, Jenna was knocked to the ground. The rain poured all around her, distorting her sight.

As the shock of the fall set in, she screamed. "NO!" In a frantic frenzy, she scrambled to her feet.

The cat closed in.

"You can't have him!" she shrieked.

Charlie remained behind her legs as she backed away from the cat. He began to yelp and whimper. Jenna recognized the desperate sounds—Biscuit had made them also, on the night he tried to attack her. "Please—no! She said you wouldn't hurt us!"

The cat stopped and looked at her in a peculiar manner.

The blaring blast of the rifle once again filled the wet air. Jenna turned, she could see her father's face.

When she looked back, the cat was gone. She couldn't understand it; the cat's eyes were familiar, somehow. The flame-driven red had faded into green. *It can't be!*

She felt the spot where the cat had hit her. There were no cuts, no slices, no marks. The cat hadn't used its claws, and Jenna wondered why.

She was comforted by happy grunts as Charlie began to paw at her leg.

Bending down, she hugged him. He lifted his furry head and licked her face. Jenna checked him over for injuries but couldn't find any.

The rain tapered off as her father approached. "Jenna, are you okay?"

"Yeah, I'm okay, and Charlie's fine—he hasn't been touched."

"Are you sure?" He bent down and gave the dog a thorough feel.

"Dad, he's fine." Her eyes scanned the cornfield. When she first arrived on the scene, the cat was waiting at the edge of the backyard. It seemed disturbed by the fact that Charlie was inside the field.

Her father looked disapprovingly at her. "What were you thinking, Jenna? That's a wild animal out there. You could have been seriously injured or even killed!"

"Dad—I'm sorry. I was just worried about Charlie."

"I don't want to hear it. Let's just get back to the house," he said, sharply.

Together, they ran through the yard.

Jenna's mother was waiting at the back door with dry towels. "Is everyone all right?"

"We're fine, Barbara. It's just our daughter we have to worry about."

Jenna's mother crossed her arms and followed them into the kitchen. "So, first you tell us that you're going to Tamara's house but instead you disappear. Then, we find you walking in the middle of a dark street, in the pouring rain, no less, where you almost got hit. And then you go chasing after a wild animal without thinking. What's going on with you, Jenna?"

"Mom—I'm sorry," she said, touching her head. "I've had a rough day. And all I wanted to do was protect Charlie, is that so wrong?"

Her mother removed an ice pack from the freezer and pressed it against Jenna's head. "You're missing the point—why did you lie about going to Tamara's house?"

Jenna thought for a moment. "I didn't want you to worry about me. I went to the museum."

"The museum? Why didn't you just tell us?"

"Because I didn't want Grandma to know. She would've asked you where I went . . . and well . . . it's a long story."

Her mother sighed. "How's your head feeling?"

"Sore, but better."

"Look, I'm sorry for the drill, but you gave us both quite the scare tonight. Why don't you go take a bath and get into some dry clothes. We'll talk after."

"Okay," Jenna nodded.

On leaving the room, she heard her mother say, "We should call someone, Reid, and let them know that something's out there."

Jenna fought the urge to go running back in. She had worried her parents enough for one day. They didn't need to add 'crazy' and 'lunatic' to the list. Besides, they would never believe that Grandma Abby was living in the body of an ancient, field-dwelling feline. Jenna had a hard enough time believing it herself.

With great effort, she climbed up the stairs to her room.

Jenna was tired, wet, sore and hungry. Every part of her body was in utter disarray. She felt empty, drained of all her emotions.

Ted and Tony were asleep on the bed when she opened the door. Everything now was quiet.

Outside the window, the sky was cloudless. The moon hung low, like a protective mother keeping close watch. Jenna looked off towards the cornfield. Things seemed so placid now.

Slanting her head, she saw the small star dangling down. It represented the Star of Omandai, she was sure of that now. It looked exactly like the drawing inside the mummy's case. Jenna also figured that her grandmother was the one who put it there, she just didn't know why.

After breaking her gaze from the star, she left and headed for the bathroom. The white porcelain tub was calling her name.

She turned on the taps and sat on the floor, then pulled the map from her pocket while waiting for the water to rise. *Is the other half of the star really underneath our cornfield?*

Her fingers brushed over the warm water. It felt good. She turned off the taps and rested for a moment with her back against the tub. *Dr. Osiris will be looking for this,* she thought. *And soon he'll be coming for it.*

Jenna wasn't too sure where this adventure would take her tomorrow. But right now, she wanted to relax. A nice, hot bath was the way to achieve that.

* * *

Twenty minutes later, Jenna opened the bathroom door. With the speed of a tortoise, she plodded towards her bedroom. She was drying her hair with a towel when she heard loud voices downstairs.

Leaning over the railing, she saw a tall, thin man standing at the front door, yelling at her mother. It was Peter, Dr. Osiris's son.

His voice was manic; the neighbours could probably hear him ranting. Jenna assumed that he had come for the missing map.

Instantly, she got chills.

He paced in the hallway, waving his hands madly about in the air. But Jenna was surprised at the words coming out of his mouth.

"I need to get into the museum tonight, Barbara. Mike was there today and he left something behind, something very valuable. It's important that I get it back."

Jenna's mother shook her head. "I'm sorry, Peter, but I can't do that. It was different when your father was the curator, but he's not there anymore. You'll have to wait until the museum opens in the morning. Anyway, I'm busy with Reid right now at the clinic. I can't leave him."

Peter was infuriated by her response. "Fine! But you better watch out because I'll be back, and next time it won't be for the key!" He threw open the door and slammed it as he left.

Jenna's mother held her chest for a moment.

"Mom—are you okay?" Jenna said, racing down the stairs. She was quite concerned.

"I'm fine, Jenna. I'll be right back." She ran down the hallway and out the back door.

What a jerk, Jenna thought. She wondered if Dr. Osiris was responsible for Peter's visit to their house. She just couldn't believe that the old man was involved with any of this; he seemed so innocent. It made sense, though. His transformation from archaeologist to farmer was so bizarre. Now, she knew why. He needed their land to find the Star of Omandai.

Standing at the bottom of the stairs, Jenna strummed her fingers along the railing. As the moments passed, she devised a plan of her own. At daybreak, she would search for the ruby. And with the cornfield in mind, she had a pretty good idea of where to start.

MYSTERIOUS DISAPPEARANCE

enna stood by the bedroom window, looking up at the sky. She couldn't sleep, the weather outside wouldn't let her. The wind grew in strength as it wrestled with the trees. Something was coming.

Her alarm clock said two-thirty in the morning but it could've been six a.m. for all she cared. Either way, she was going to be sleep deprived. The stars are what she noticed now, brightly crowded in the night sky. The wind had forced the clouds away, leaving nothing but twinkling blackness.

Jenna turned her attention to the cornfield. A dim light now moved inside of it. In her mind, it looked like the dorsal fin of a hungry rogue shark searching for dinner. Only its fin surfaced above the field. It wasn't of course, it was just her imagination. What she saw was a light moving back and forth. But the way it was moving, is what held her focus.

Quietly, she opened the window. *What is that?* The stalks tilted from side to side in an odd, convulsive manner.

Although Jenna was hesitant to go outside alone in the dark, she wanted to see what the light was. Her thrill-seeking side was quickly overriding her sense of caution.

She dressed herself, left the bedroom and tiptoed down the stairs. She stopped in the kitchen and collected a flashlight from one of the drawers. Just as she was about to open the back door, a noise came from the floor. Peering down, she saw Charlie following her.

"No way, Mister. You're not going out there. You've had enough fun for one night." She found some treats on the counter and bent down to feed him. Charlie wiggled his tail about. "Charlie, you're a wonderful guard dog, but even you could have been really hurt today. Now, go back upstairs," she pointed towards the hallway. "Upstairs, Mister!"

He finished his biscuits and left.

Jenna searched the kitchen for any other midnight wanderers. With no other stragglers in tow, she exited the house and made her way towards the cornfield. The light from the crop was still visible in the dark, but just barely.

When she reached the edge of the yard, she stopped and took a deep confidence-building breath. Then, with all the courage she could assemble, she stepped through the first row of stalks.

Jenna was impressed with herself. For the moment, she was controlled, almost gallant, considering what happened the last time she entered the field at night. But regardless of that, her emotions were strong. Pursuit of an answer—that's what drove her.

Feeling her head, there were no lumps or bumps. Just the natural arc of her forehead. *Thank God,* she thought.

Slowly, her body migrated through the field as she swept away the stalks with her hands. She carried on until there was no trace of the farm behind her.

Suddenly, her feet came to a standstill. Directly ahead of her was an open space; a small clearing in the middle of the field. The cornstalks had been removed. It wasn't large enough to cause worry from the perspective of the house, and it certainly wasn't anything her father would agonize over.

The stalks had been tossed aside, which was strange since they appeared to be healthy. *Why would someone remove good corn?* Jenna knew the answer, she just didn't want to admit it.

Leaning over, she surveyed the ground. The soil was dark and moist. Although it had rained earlier, the ground everywhere else had dried up. The dirt where she was standing looked as though it had been freshly turned.

Initially, it was the light that had roused Jenna's suspicions and motivated her to visit the field. *Where is it now?* She gazed around the clearing but saw no light other than the one she was holding in her hand.

Her eyes then came across something a few feet away. A weak ray emitted from the ground. She moved closer and brushed away the soil that covered it. A large flashlight now pointed straight up into the sky. "That's random," she scoffed.

The tips of her fingers came across something else. A feeling of dread sank deep inside of her when she realized what it was. "This is part of Dr. Osiris's sweater."

Her head twitched from side to side as she now understood the relevance. "Oh no . . ."

Stepping back from the fabric, she felt something hard beneath her foot. Pointing the flashlight, she moved aside. Something else was protruding from the ground. She didn't want to touch it, but spurred herself on.

She cleared the soil away and gently felt the object. "Ahh!" she screamed and stumbled backwards. A cold, lifeless hand was sticking out.

Her arms quivered as she forced the light onto the spot. A gold lion ring twinkled in the gleam of the flashlight. Her stomach started to flip. "Oh my God!"

As she turned to flee, something seized her ankle. Jenna screeched and fell to the ground. The flashlight dropped from her hand and rolled out of reach. Her arms swatted madly about, trying to break from the hold. With one swift kick of her other leg, she was released.

She quickly crawled over to the flashlight, pointed it at the soil and stared in disbelief. The hand was fighting to free itself.

"Dr. Osiris!" she cried. "I'm sorry, I'm sorry!" She raced over, interlocked her fingers with his and pulled with all her might.

Then suddenly, the earth began to move.

In a wild panic, she pulled even harder. Everything about this night was wrong. Everything. Jenna could feel his hand slipping from her grasp. "No—don't give up! I'll get you out!"

But in one sporadic motion, his hand was sucked into the ground.

"NO!" Jenna burst into tears.

Her sadness was stifled, when the soil from the clearing rose into a monstrous earth-driven fury. The winds lifted the hair off of her shoulders as they twisted faster and faster in the form of a tornado. Jenna couldn't believe what was happening.

Boosted by fear, she turned on her heels and tore through the field. She ran without stopping, and did not look back.

Her emotions were divided, littered everywhere. She was horrified, angry, frustrated, burdened. Tears slid down her cheeks as she ran for the house.

Upon reaching the backyard, she slowed down and gasped for air. Jenna had never been so terrified in her life. Had she waited a moment longer, she probably would have been sucked into a swirling grave. Her body swaggered towards the house as she struggled to regulate her breathing.

When her feet touched the wood of the first porch stair, her heart began to calm. Distance was now her shield.

Looking back, she saw the eyes of the Siamese cat staring at her from the edge of the cornfield.

"Dr. Osiris—" she sobbed. "What have you done with him?"

The animal ignored her. It turned and disappeared into the stalks. It had claimed its victim. Jenna knew that soon, it would be hunting for another.

She had to stop it.

With tears muddling her sight, she climbed the stairs. She couldn't fathom why Dr. Osiris had gone out there at night. It was the first time that she ever saw him in the field. *He must have come to find the Star of Omandai.*

A thrill of anger swept over her as she gathered her senses. Whatever his reasons, if Dr. Osiris believed that the star was on their property, then so did Jenna. She came to the conclusion that she would need to return to the cornfield. Evil thoughts wormed and wriggled in her head at the idea. She had qualms about even getting close to it. But it had to be done. Her trepidation prevented her from re-entering at night, so she decided to wait until morning before venturing back in. It would be safest then, she figured. Daylight would protect her.

Just then, the kitchen light turned on. "Jenna, is that you?" a drowsy voice came from inside. The door opened and her mother stepped out onto the porch.

"Yes, it's me. I didn't mean to wake you. I just came outside for some fresh air." She wiped the wetness from her eyes.

"It's okay, I was in the clinic. Sweetie, you've been crying—what's wrong?"

"Oh, nothing. I was just thinking of my friends back home. I miss them sometimes." Jenna hoped that her mother believed her phony act. Right now, she didn't feel like divulging any secrets.

"Are you sure?"

"Yes, I'm sure. How's everything at the clinic? How are the animals?"

"Everyone's stable. We haven't lost anyone, yet," she said in a sombre tone. "Your father's a mess, though. He's been working day and night out there."

"Where is he now?"

"He's resting in the clinic. I came to make him something to eat."

Jenna followed her mother into the house. "I'm glad they're okay."

"We're lucky, I guess," her mother said, turning on the coffee pot. "Do you want something to drink? I can make you some tea."

"Actually, I'm really tired, Mom. I think I'm ready for bed now." With slow steps she headed for the hallway.

Her mother stopped her before she could leave. "Jenna, is there something you're not telling me?"

She turned and shook her head. "No—why?"

"I don't know. It seems like you're hiding something. Are you?"

Jenna looked out the window towards the cornfield. "No," she said. "Not in this house."

BEFORE YOU LOSE

The alarm came to life at six o'clock in the morning. Lying on her stomach, Jenna slammed down her hand to turn it off. She had slept only two hours. Her intention was to have pulled an all-nighter, but her body longed for rest.

When she moved, a heavy weight shifted on her back. She lifted her right arm and felt two tails, dangling.

Jenna moaned. "Sorry, boys, but your bed needs to get up." Both cats capered to the ground as she rolled over.

Half-awake and sluggish, she sat up and yawned. Although a slight discomfort, Jenna had slept in her clothes to save herself some time. She opened the drawer of the bedside table, took out the map and placed it in her pants pocket. Then silently, she left her room and went downstairs to the kitchen to consume her breakfast.

Ten minutes later, after filling her belly, Jenna stepped outside into the crisp morning air. It helped wake her. She took a deep breath and began to make her way towards the cornfield. Her heart picked up speed with each step that she took. Passing by the picnic blanket, she stopped. It was once again removed from the hole. Immediately, she turned her attention to the skeleton. The bones were back in the ground.

Jenna let out a grateful sigh. For the moment, her fears were mollified.

Neither her Mom nor Dad had mentioned anything about the hole or the skeleton, so Jenna assumed that they hadn't seen it. Even when her father came out with his rifle, he hadn't said anything. And when they ran back to the house together, Jenna had led her father away from the hole. It was just one more needless worry for him. She tried to protect him from that.

Looking straight ahead, she knew that today would be quite the challenge, returning to the scene of some otherworldly crime. But if it meant finding out what happened to Dr. Osiris, then she was willing to push forth.

As she approached the outermost layer of stalks, she instructed her feet to take a breather. The mass of corn now took on a different appearance. They looked almost military in form, like a tall regiment of green and yellow warriors.

A whirling whisper came from behind them. Jenna thought that she heard voices, screams maybe. Every muscle in her body except one, was in accordance: given the signal they would work as a conglomerate to take her safely back to the house. But her brain opposed. "Mind over matter, right?" she encouraged herself.

Clenching her hands, she stepped into the field.

Today, she was slightly overwhelmed by the size of the stalks; she felt quite small in the midst of them. Continuing on, she moved the giant leaves with her hands as she walked from row to row. Up ahead, was the clearing. The sky started to dim when she moved towards it. Clouds now encircled the sun, blocking the rays with moisture. *Uh oh . . .*

During her night visit, Jenna noticed that the soil had been disturbed. She thought that Dr. Osiris might have been digging there. But when that strange twister appeared, it moved all the dirt, leaving no trace of anything.

Quickly, she pulled the map from her pocket and unfolded it. The legend in the corner showed three different ground layers; each designated by a small, coloured box. The top box was light brown—representing soil. The middle box was dark brown, indicating richer soil. Then, she saw the bottom box. It was white, with 'sand' written beside it.

"That's ridiculous! Sand beneath the soil . . . beneath a cornfield?" Jenna looked at the ground and then at the map. "There's no sand here!"

When she returned the paper to her pocket, she detected a slight depression in the ground. It was roughly where she had found Dr. Osiris. Her thoughts soured. But she reminded herself that she wouldn't allow her emotions to bury her. Not right now, anyway.

Kneeling, she picked up a handful of soil and watched as it seeped through her fingers. A slight wind ruffled her hair, beseeching her attention. Her eyes peered through the stalks.

A whistling breeze called out her name, "Jennnnnaaaaa . . ." It had her immediate attention.

A mild tremor grew in the ground as the base of the stalks began to move. Like immobile dominoes, each one began to tremble and lean. She could sense the vibration, there was no mistaking it. Without having to look, she knew that the sky had turned black. *Oh no* . . .

And then she heard it.

A resounding roar came from behind her. Jenna was now afraid.

The cornstalks shifted in place as the lone hunter made its way towards her. Jenna knew exactly what was coming. It was a trap, and she had walked right into it.

SANDTRAP

Jenna's body struggled to function as she looked for a way out. The vibration in the ground was getting closer. She could take a chance and try to outrun the Siamese cat, but soon realized that that was no longer an option.

Now, standing in the clearing, was the feline menace. Its head was low and its jaws were open. Jenna suspended all activity, not a single muscle moved.

Its powerful legs brought it closer towards her. Its predatory stance was commanding, deserving of her full attention.

"You don't want to hurt me," she said, in a desperate plea.

The earth was now quiet. There was no vibration, no rumble. The cornstalks were motionless.

Jenna watched the animal breathe. It seemed distressed, angered that she had tried to fool it.

It stopped approximately five feet from where she was standing.

Jenna was absolutely appalled. She had nowhere to go. *I'm going to die*, was the only thought that she had.

Surprisingly, she was given a moment's reprieve when the cat's massive paws began to move in front of her. Its sleek, brawny body paced steadily, back and forth.

Why isn't it attacking? Jenna thought that the animal's behaviour was unusual. She half-expected to be dead already. It seemed as though the cat was waiting for something, or someone. *God, what's going to happen to me?*

Suddenly, something tugged at her jeans. Jenna screamed when she saw two arms reaching up through the soil. Each one wrapped around her legs and pulled her into the ground. The soil swirled like a funnel as her body dropped lower and lower. Everything was happening so fast. "Someone—help me!" she yelled out.

Terrified of the unknown, horrified by her capture, she frantically grasped at the ground around her. She opened her mouth to scream but her lungs filled up with soil. The air was disappearing, she was drowning in the earth. Tears poured down her face. She wailed uncontrollably when realizing her fate.

The cornstalks now watched her like large, faceless witnesses. She looked up at them for some form of help, but they soon faded from her view. Her eyes began to shut. A cool sensation overcame her as she slipped into a deep sleep. Within seconds, her entire body was swallowed into the ground. All that was left on the surface was the soil, the air, and the tall, silent stalks.

The sun broke through the darkness and there was once again, a bright, beautiful blue sky.

WHAT LIES BENEATH

ne eye opened first and then the other followed, that's how Jenna regained her sight. She lay on her back staring at the cold, dank air.

A strange inner tickling moved up and down her body. Her limbs tingled, her head buzzed—every part of her was in sensory overload. She was alive. *Oh, thank God!*

She sat up slowly, coughed and spit out a mouthful of soil. She put her hands on her throat and massaged it gently. *What happened? Where am I?* She hacked over and over, until the discharging soil ran out.

Placing her hands back down, she touched the ground. A soft, crystal material lay beneath her. It felt out of place, foreign. Jenna brushed her fingers along the floor and picked up a handful of sand. She remembered the map of the fields—the sub-lying layer was sand. White sand. Just like the desert that surrounded King Odon's temple.

Jenna's head was dizzy. She fumbled in the dark as she tried to stand. Something by her feet nearly made her fall. Feeling it, she realized that it was the flashlight she'd found in the soil, lying next to Dr. Osiris. It was now off. Finding the switch, she turned it on. It worked, but was slowly dying.

From the stream of dim light, Jenna could see that she had fallen into a cave. It had a ghostly feel to it, like a lost mission or Indian burial ground.

Gazing up, she pointed the flashlight at the ceiling. "Of course there's no opening! How did I get in here, then?" There was no entrance anywhere that Jenna could see.

Tracing the walls with the light, she noticed something on them. Various designs were painted on the rock. "Those look like . . . drawings . . . old drawings." The walls were covered with golden images. "Wow—this is beautiful!"

Stepping back, Jenna viewed them all. Each one registered immediately when she saw it. As a collective, the drawings showed the story of Menao and the Siamese Mummy. She was completely entranced, immersed in the tale, so much that she wasn't paying attention to anything else.

"Jennnnaaaaaa . . ." a wispy voice called out.

Her body jolted alive. She held the flashlight protectively in front of her. "Who's there?"

There was no reply, just silence.

"I said—who's there?" She was starting to feel less and less alone. Her anxious fingers moved the flashlight around the cave in all directions.

Soft words filled the air. "Follow the lighted path . . . ."

Jenna hesitated, but followed the instructions. Turning off the flashlight, she looked around the cave. A dusky orange glow lit the path in front of her. It seemed to be leading to another part of the cave. Cautiously, she walked towards the light. Her body was being lured deeper into the unknown.

Jenna tracked the light as it led her past a long hallway of rock.

"Jennnnnaaaa . . . helppppp . . . usssss," she heard in the hallway.

She stopped to listen. Her nervous system was in high gear. Regardless of that fact, her body began to move forward, against her better judgement. Jenna felt like she was on automatic pilot.

Up ahead, the hallway opened up into another spacious, dark-walled area. She took control of her feet and hid behind a giant boulder by the entrance. Lifting her head, she peered into the cave. Jenna couldn't believe what she saw. Broad stone pillars with amber globes sitting atop of them were strewn across the floor. At the far end of the room was a monstrous black and white statue, standing proud. It was breathtaking.

Jenna recognized her surroundings. She was inside King Odon's temple.

Then, something moved in front of her. She crouched down, revealing only her eyes. She watched as the Siamese cat slinked in and out from behind the pillars, staring at the walls as it passed by them. Around the cave it drifted, while its eyes focused on the rocky perimeter.

And then Jenna saw them. Lining the walls were hundreds of mummified bodies. Lying in front of them, were several human-sized coffins. Jenna was astounded; this part was new.

In the middle of the room sat a large, stone sarcophagus. It was open with nothing inside of it.

A blaring roar filled the cave and at once Jenna knew that the Siamese cat had found her. It glared at her behind the rock. Her body cowered and trembled in place. Jenna closed her eyes and wished the cat away. When she opened them, it had disappeared.

She flew out of hiding when a frightening growl came from behind her. With its fearsome presence, it forced Jenna out into the open.

Desperately, she looked around the cave for some form of protection, but there was none. As a last resort, she threw the flashlight at the cat.

It roared back and continued on towards her. Although it was steering her into the room, it wasn't attacking. That's when she realized—it was pushing her towards the sarcophagus.

Jenna shook her head. "Oh, no. I'm not going in there!"

The room filled with activity as each of the mummies awoke. With their arms held stiffly in front of them, they dragged themselves towards Jenna. Strategically, they formed a circle around her as the cat backed away and watched.

"No—get away from me!" she kicked and screamed.

Showing no emotion, they closed in on all sides like a uniformed league.

Jenna didn't understand what was going on. Her feet floundered as she spun around to protect herself. She stumbled onto the floor and howled. Ragged white linens now surrounded her on every side. She tried to turn away, but was compelled to look into their eyes. *Eyes! The mummies have eyes!*

She recognized one of her captors—Dr. Osiris. He looked at her with an absent expression. Then suddenly it hit her like a fast train: the mummies were the people who had disappeared.

Feeling their hands now upon her, Jenna's cries climbed an octave. "No! No! PLEASE—NO!"

They lifted her up and carried her towards the sarcophagus. She pleaded and begged to be released.

Without any form of acknowledgement, they hauled her body over to the stone coffin. Jenna coiled and thrashed about as she tried to escape, but couldn't break free from the multitude of hands that enveloped her.

She was now being lowered into the sarcophagus. "NO!" Her voice was shrill and hurting, but still she screamed with volume. Three of the mummies pressed down on her arms, legs and torso. Jenna looked up and saw the eyes of someone she hadn't expected to see.

Worse than that, a large, stone lid now loomed above her. They were sealing her in.

The arms withdrew as the lid was placed on top. Jenna wailed inside the closed coffin. "Let me out! Don't do this! Please—somebody help me!"

She pressed her knees up against the stone cover and pushed with every bit of strength that she had. Nothing. Then she tried to move it with her arms. Nothing. "Let me out—PLEASE!" Rolling onto her stomach, she pushed with her back. It was unmovable. Jenna collapsed face down. Her body was exhausted. But although her energy levels were low, her sense of survival was strong.

She flipped over onto her back and pressed her arms and knees against the top. With all her might, she pushed. "Please—let me out of here!"

Delirium suddenly shot through her veins. Her eyes were now manic, her body enraged. She began to claw madly at the stone. "GET ME OUT OF HERE!" Her knuckles bled and her fingernails broke, but none of that mattered now.

She finally lost all composure and began to punch uncontrollably at the stone. Each strike came with a hysterical scream.

With every gulp of air, her breath was fading. No one was going to rescue her. Tears streamed down her face. "Please," she sobbed. "Let me out! I can't die like this!"

Her heart began to shut down as her body succumbed to the weakness.

Then, something unexpected happened. The bottom of the coffin gave way and Jenna fell out into darkened space. Too tired to do anything else, she let her body go limp. Painless and peaceful, relaxed and free, Jenna remained in a safe place exempt from harshness and captivity. But that was not to last.

WHAM! With a heavy blow, she was brought back to reality. Jenna had landed.

Opening her eyes, she winced in pain. Her right arm was squished beneath the weight of her body. She rolled onto her back and held it close. "Ahh!"

Blue sky hovered above her; the sun was now exposed. Flopping her head from side to side, Jenna saw that she had landed inside the cornfield.

Her only desire at that moment was to sleep. She wanted to lay down her head and never wake up—she was in that much pain.

Many minutes passed and she remained horizontal. But then her mind caught up with her. Realistically, if this wasn't a dream and her arm was truly injured, then it would have to be treated. But no doctor would ever see it. Jenna would have to fix it herself. There was no way she would ever go to a hospital voluntarily.

Gently, she peeled herself off of the ground. Her eyes squinted in the sunlight. Her internal compass was broken, so she cupped her eyes and viewed the sun's location in the sky. After gathering her bearings, she turned and walked through the stalks.

Tears accompanied her thoughts now. Below the cornfield, Jenna saw something that tore at her heart. Something horrifying, something close to home. Her mother—her very own mother—had been taken captive below the field. Jenna knew it when she saw her eyes.

Anger and exasperation merged together to quell the fear in her system. Prompted by determination, she overcame her woes. Jenna wasn't going to give up, especially not now. There was a time and a place for surrender, but this wasn't it. Now, more than ever, Jenna was going to persevere.

Looking down at her bloodied knuckles and broken nails, she gasped. Her injuries were frightening—but were also disappearing. Her nails grew back and the blood evaporated right before her eyes. Only her arm hurt. It was throbbing, but that would have to be kept a secret from her family.

As Jenna made her way home, she thought about the cave below the cornfield and the ruby she never found. And she couldn't understand why she'd been released when all the others had been captured. The only answer she could come up with, was that the Siamese cat needed her to find the Star of Omandai. *But if it's not under the cornfield, then where is it?* she wondered.

Jenna's pains were suppressed by her tenacity; she wanted to find the star and end the curse of the Siamese Mummy.

She remembered when Peter had stopped by their house to get the key for the museum. He said that Michael had left something there. Jenna did some mental arithmetic. *If Michael was the man I saw in the museum, then Peter probably wanted access to the back room so that he could get his hands on the box.* It made sense to Jenna. All three men wanted the Star of Omandai; all three desired a great fortune.

She was also under the impression that Michael had disappeared. The puzzle pieces were fitting into place.

During her visit with Dr. Osiris, he had received a phone call. Jenna figured that the call was from Michael. She assumed that he'd told his father about the missing box. And Peter was in the room listening. Then, Michael disappeared.

And that's when she finally understood the situation. Dr. Osiris wasn't looking for the Star of Omandai in the cornfield. He was there for another reason.

He was looking for Michael!

THE STAR OF OMANDAI

The Star of Omandai was what this story was truly about. Those who had disappeared without a trace, had left behind loved ones that were desperate to find them. Sick and diseased animals were entrusted into the hands of those who could save them, but they too, had a future that was uncertain. A giant Siamese predator was roaming the city, wreaking havoc on those who crossed its path. And inside the Lionhead Museum, tucked within its restraining linens, jailed within its glass and bars, was an ominous mastermind controlling it all.

Yet, with everything involved, there wouldn't be a mystery if it wasn't for one very special ruby: the Star of Omandai.

The protective talisman of the Siamese Mummy was a precious object, indeed. A ruby most rare and coveted. It belonged on the neck of a powerful cat and not in the hands of man. Like many other beloved objects ordained in value, the ruby had been stolen. Greed, had reared its ugly head.

For King Odon, his humble servants, his Siamese guardians and his people—life had been destroyed by greed. They would forever remember man's capacity for such misplaced passion. And for this, they would pay.

Although hope seemed unachievable, the star's fate did not lie in the hearts of sinful men. Severed as it was, it would come together under the hands of one courageous act.

Part had already been found, the wheels of change were in motion. The rest lay in waiting for the day that a young woman would find it. And there, it remained, under the most unsuspecting of places.

TIME IS ESCAPING

Jenna sat on the edge of her bed with a large icepack pressed against her forearm. The pain had narrowed but not subsided as she had hoped. It wasn't broken though, which pleased her, incredibly. She knew what that felt like.

Her wrist had become quite swollen however, and that worried her. But Jenna was a strong girl and could withstand a lot of agony without complaint. Right now, she had to. Her mind drifted back to her mother. She reached for a tissue as her cheeks prepared for the outpouring of dribble.

Her mother's whereabouts was another secret she had to keep, which is why she wanted to end this story as soon as possible. Jenna wanted her mother back. That kind of grief, she couldn't take.

It was now three o'clock in the afternoon. She looked over at Ted and Tony who were just waking up from a snooze. "You guys must be hungry," she said, wiping her eyes. Ted walked onto her lap and started kneading her leg like a piece of dough. Tony promenaded behind her, rubbing his head against her shirt.

Gazing over at the bedroom window, Jenna stared at the red crystal star. It reminded her of the drawing inside the mummy's case. The star was surrounded by a circle of braided flowers. As if someone had hit her on the head with a rolling pin, it suddenly occurred to her. "I know that design!"

She set down the icepack and shifted Ted to the bed. She walked over to the window and opened it with her good arm. Her eyes were looking for something specific. Leaning through, she saw what she was searching for. "The garden!" Hidden behind the bushes was her grandmother's herb and spice garden. And like a ring that bound two people together, the garden was protected by a spherical perimeter of red and white roses.

An image of a large star reflected back in Jenna's eyes. "I don't believe it! All this time—the garden was a sign! That's why Grandma hung the crystal there." She paused and thought for a moment. "Is the other half of the Star of Omandai buried beneath the garden?" Jenna had to find out.

She looked over at the cats. "Come on, boys. We've got work to do!"

Jenna headed downstairs to the kitchen. She made sure that her sleeve was covering her arm when she walked into the room. Her father was on the telephone, and the dogs were at their food dishes. Without drawing too much attention to herself, she decided to feed the cats first and then go outside.

Removing the box of cat food from the cupboard, she heard her father yell.

"A person just doesn't go missing without any trace!" His voice then calmed. "I'm sorry, you're right. I'm jumping to conclusions. Maybe she went into town for something. It's just that she wouldn't have left without telling me."

He looked like he hadn't slept in days. But Jenna knew that he'd been working nonstop since the day Mr. Winters brought Calvin in.

"Yeah, thanks, Nick. If you see her, let me know. Sorry I yelled."

Jenna poured the cat food into the dishes and placed them on the floor. The two felines sauntered into the kitchen to eat. "Dad—what's going on?" she said, looking at the dark circles beneath his eyes.

He waited, and then spoke. "I don't know how to say this, Jenna, but . . . your mother is missing. I don't know where she went and I'm worried. She never takes off without telling anyone. I tried Nick at the lab but he hasn't seen her. I called the neighbours. I called the museum. No one's seen her. I don't know where she is."

"I don't understand—I just saw Mom this morning, right here in the kitchen."

He stared blankly at her. "Jenna, you couldn't have. You've been at Tamara's house the last three nights. Your grandmother took you there, remember?"

Jenna was severely confused. "*What?* What day is this?"

He began to walk towards the front door. "It's Saturday, Jenna. Your brother comes home today. And if he calls, don't tell him anything about your mother. He doesn't need to worry. Just tell him that everything is fine, and that I'll pick him up at the airport when his flight comes in tonight. I'm going to look for your mother. Take care of the house while I'm gone."

Jenna began to fret; her father was acting so rash. "But what about the clinic? What about the animals?"

"Nick's on his way over to take care of things. He'll be here any minute. I'm sorry, Jenna. I have to go." He rushed out the door before she could say anything else.

She followed and watched as he got into the car, backed out of the driveway and sped off down the street.

Three days? she thought. *I've been gone for three days?* Jenna couldn't believe it. And now her mother was gone, her father was searching for her, and her grandmother was telling lies. *This family needs my help!*

Jenna knew where her mother was. She wished that there was some way to impart that information to her father without sounding like a total loon.

But Jenna was more worried about her grandmother. *Why would she tell Dad that I was at Tamara's house, when I wasn't?* She looked up the stairs towards her grandmother's room. Her concerns were running rampant: fear, distrust, denial, disorientation. Like the limbs of a tree, her emotions were all branching from one particular family member.

Jenna finally accepted her grandmother's secret—she just didn't want to think about it. All the arrows however, were pointing in her direction. *Grandma must have known that I was in the cave—because she was in the cave.*

For Jenna, it seemed as though she'd been underground for a short period of time, but almost three days had passed in the world above her. Above ground, her mother was missing. Below ground, she was trapped in the cave, wrapped in white linen and held against her will, along with the rest of the people who had disappeared from the city.

Her body may have been concealed but there was no mistaking her eyes. She was one of the mummies who held Jenna's body down inside the sarcophagus.

Time was of the essence. Jenna had to hurry and find the star if she wanted all of this to end.

She ran through the hallway and climbed down the basement stairs. She came back up holding a small shovel in her hand.

The back door flew open as she jumped down the porch stairs and raced towards the garden.

The bushes were her only hurdle now. Carefully, she made her way through them as she held her injured arm tight to her body. Her wrist was pulsating. Ignoring the pain, she directed all of her attention towards the garden. Arriving on the other side, she stopped. Planted right in front of her feet, were the roses.

Jenna looked up at the star hanging in her bedroom window. She then stepped through the protective layer of red and white flowers and bent down to look at the garden. These were the ingredients for her grandmother's specially formulated herbal concoctions. This was her mixing lab. Jenna leaned over to breathe it all in. The fragrant aromas were illuminating her senses.

"Focus, Jenna. Focus," she told herself.

A loud thump came from the side of the house. Peeking through the bushes, Jenna saw Nick leaving his car to go inside the clinic. She was glad that he was there, and felt comforted by his presence.

Turning back, she redirected her concentration. With the shovel ready for action, she began to dig.

* * *

Jenna's hands had been in the soil for almost twenty minutes when the head of the shovel hit something hard in the ground. Removing the dirt, she smiled. A small, red box had been unearthed. She picked it up and quickly stood. It looked just like the black box from the museum; same size, same shape, same glisten.

On the front of the box, was a keyhole. Jenna hoped that the key hidden upstairs in her room would open this box as well.

Holding it securely in her hand, she pushed her way through the bushes and gazed around the yard. Everything was quiet, still-like. Lifting her head, she watched the clouds move in front of the sun. "Uh oh . . ."

The sky grew dark in a threatening manner. Rain started to fall all around. Somewhere in the distance thunder rumbled. "I better get out of here!"

But before she even took a step, lightning struck the cornfield. A shockwave rippled over the ground sending Jenna a clear message—the cat was coming for her.

She fell backwards as the earth-driven wave swept beneath her feet. The box dropped from her hand and landed in the grass. Immediately, she grabbed it and stood. A deep-throated bellow carried across the yard. Looking at the cornfield, Jenna saw the Siamese cat now rushing towards her. Its body ran with vicious intent.

Without hesitation, Jenna charged towards the back door of the house. Heavy rain now emptied from the sky above her, attacking her with every drop. She leapt up the porch stairs and slammed into the door. Her body doubled over. "Jesus . . ." she cried, holding her arm. There was no time. Disregarding the pain, her hand twisted around the doorknob.

Inside, all three dogs were barking and scratching hysterically at the door to get out. If it opened, then all the animals would escape and she'd really be in trouble.

Behind her, the cat was quickly approaching.

Jenna hustled down the stairs and darted towards the front of the house, through the gushing rain. She remembered that the front door was unlocked.

When she turned her head to see where the cat was, she slipped on the wet lawn. The box flew out of her hand and cascaded down to the ground. Her body then landed with a grievous force. "Ahh!" She had fallen onto her injured arm.

Jenna wailed in agony as she rolled onto her back. Her arm was now limp; it was definitely broken. Anguish flooded her, she wanted to give up. Nothing was worth this much pain. *Let it be done with*, she thought. *Let it be over.*

Her mind began to float in and out of consciousness. Time began to rewind. She could see herself at the age of ten, climbing down from the tree house. Her shoes skidded out from beneath her body and she plummeted to the ground.

Jenna remembered that she had been so careful descending the ladder. *Why again, did I fall?*

She lay on the ground, watching the scene play over in her mind. Looking up at the small, wooden house, she saw something hiding in the branches of the Maple tree next to it. Terrified and vocal, it was the neighbor's Siamese cat. It was stuck. Jenna had left the tree house to get her father's help. The cat had hissed, growled and swatted at her, startling her, causing her to lose her balance. That's why she fell. *The cat made me fall.*

Her younger self stood over her now. "Get up, Jenna," she whispered. "You can beat this, don't give up . . ." The girl's arms appeared above her. "Take my hands, I will help you."

Jenna felt herself reaching for them.

Then, in a swirling motion of time, she was brought back to the present moment. A surge of hope infiltrated her body. Her eyes popped open. Swiftly, she shielded them from the rain. Her voyage to the house was not that far. The front porch stairs were close. *I can do this!*

The cat roared from the side of the house, it was just around the corner. Jenna prayed that Nick and the other animals were safely protected inside the clinic.

Sitting up, she reached for the box beside her and wrapped it in her shirt. She then stood, held her injured arm close to her body and bolted towards the stairs.

Her body heaved up the steps as she opened the door and burst through to the other side.

Closing it immediately, she locked it.

Suddenly, a loud bang pulsated through the door. Jenna jumped back in surprise. The cat was trying to get in.

She shrieked when the dogs came tearing towards the front door. They all stood in front of her trying to get at the wild animal on the other side.

Jenna braced the aches in her arm—it throbbed uncontrollably. Her fear of the cat however, overpowered the damage she had done to her body.

The noise then disappeared from outside. Jenna waited a moment and then stepped closer to the front door. She peered out the window. Turning back, she saw something move out of the corner of her eye. The cat was now in front of the family room window. It paced alongside it, looking for a way in. It caught sight of Jenna and growled.

"That's it!" Jenna hollered. "Everyone upstairs!"

She herded the dogs up the stairs and locked them inside her parent's room. They beckoned at the door to be released but Jenna ignored them. Then, she called for the cats. "Ted! Tony! Where are you?"

Two meows came from inside her bedroom.

Jenna ran into the room and saw the cats perched next to the window. "Good—you guys are okay!" She closed the door behind her and collapsed onto the floor, holding her arm. The red box unfurled from her shirt. She knew that it was only a matter of time before the animal found its way inside the house. Nothing would stop it.

She stood up and walked over to the window. Directly beneath it was the Siamese cat, leering up at her. It knew where she was inside the house.

Jenna moved the cats to the floor, then secured and locked the window.

She was tired and drenched, but physically could feel nothing but the pain in her arm. She had to end this grizzly tale.

She collected the boxes and fished the key out of hiding. Gently, she lowered herself onto the floor. Holding the red box between her knees, she placed the golden key into the hole. Jenna heard a click as the lid opened.

"Yes—thank God! It worked!" Her excitement soon faded when she saw what was inside; a folded piece of black paper.

Lightning struck somewhere nearby. Jenna prepped her ears for the impending invasion of thunder.

Unfolding the paper, she saw a riddle written in gold ink.

> *'What loves you most? You do not know.*
> *To understand, your mind must grow.*
> *They hold you close, dear to their hearts,*
> *Your sacred soul and cunning smarts.*
> *Without you there, to guard and care,*
> *Their hearts will break, and gently tear.*
> *You need them more than you can know.*
> *You must look closely to see them glow.*
> *All of life will change in time,*
> *Unless you can reverse the crime.'*

Jenna was good at solving riddles, she loved them in fact. Right now her brain was boggled, but the more she read it, the more she started to comprehend its meaning. She looked back at the cats and smiled. *The cats . . .*

She was pulled out of her brain-teasing trance when she saw them once again on the windowsill, pawing at the glass.

"Boys—no! Get away from there!" She stood, rushed over and placed the cats on the bed.

At that moment, a thin stream of light penetrated the storm outside. Its path entered through the window, continued through the crystal star and flashed a dazzling red glow onto the walls. The cats chased after it as it moved around the room. Tony stood on the bed teetering on his back legs as he tried to capture the tormenting light. As he did, a second bright stream broke through the clouds. It came through the window, hit the front of his collar and bounced another red light onto the wall.

Jenna shook her head in dismay. "What is *that*?"

She reached around his neck and felt something cold and solid. Much like the star hanging from the window, a small object dangled from the base of his collar. It twinkled as she turned it. "Tony!"

Ted stood next to him, jumping at the wall. Jenna picked him up and inspected his collar. It was the same. Each cat was wearing a grape-sized jewel around its neck.

She slipped both collars off of the felines and brought them over to the boxes. Kneeling, she separated the jewels from the nylon straps and examined them thoroughly. Ted sat down on the edge of the bed and looked over her shoulder.

"Teddy—it's the Star!"

Just then, a terrifying bellow came from outside the bedroom window. Jenna screamed when she saw the cat on the roof preparing to jump in.

There was no turning back; she had to complete the task now. Returning her gaze to the floor, she placed the key into the hole of the black box. The lid opened, revealing the other half of the star.

Suddenly, the window shattered into pieces as the Siamese cat smashed through the glass and landed inside the room. Jenna was horrified. Never once did she think that she would be hunted in her own house. This was her sanctuary; the walls were not meant to be breached.

The cat turned to face the animals on the bed.

"Leave them alone!" Jenna cried. But it was too late. She watched Ted and Tony drop like flies onto the comforter. Their bodies lay motionless, in stationary positions.

"NO!" she yelled.

The Siamese cat spotted the rubies in her hand. It snapped its jaws and roared at her. The sound was hideous, and almost made her sick.

"No! You're not going to stop me!" But for some inexplicable reason, Jenna was inundated with drowsiness. Her eyes became heavy and leaden, and her body grew numb. She no longer felt the pain in her arm. The missing people, the sick animals—none of that seemed to matter. All she wanted to do was sleep.

But another voice was telling her to, "Wake up . . . wake up!"

Sitting on her bed now, was the ten-year-old Jenna. In her arms she was playing with the neighbour's Siamese cat. "See, Jenna?" she smiled. "I saved it!" She cuddled the animal as it purred beneath her fingers.

Jenna acknowledged her younger self with a nod.

"Jenna . . . it's time to wake up. Wake up, Jenna!" The girl disappeared but her words remained. "Wake up . . . wake up . . . wake up . . . WAKE UP!"

In a spastic jumble, her body awoke. Instantly, she was brought back to the hunter in her room.

Jenna shook her head at the animal as it crept towards her. "No—I won't give up! I will save you!"

The Siamese cat stopped, as if it had understood. The cat's eyes—her grandmother's eyes; they were one of the same. Everything about the story, Jenna finally accepted. Her grandmother was the soul of the Siamese Mummy.

The animal hissed and exposed its giant fangs, reminding Jenna of the war they were both entwined in. Bending on its haunches, it prepared to lunge.

With one hand, Jenna quickly gathered the pieces of the ruby. The animal sprang into the air as she fitted them into place. The ruby suddenly snapped itself together and rose up into the middle of the room. A powerful light shone through its core, forcing brilliant red beams onto every inch of the walls. Through the light, Jenna saw the Siamese cat levitating in the air above her. She screamed and lay on the floor holding her arm.

In through the window came a storm of monstrous energy. The wind gusted through the room like a fierce tornado. Jenna closed her eyes and lay flush to the floor. Her heart was engorged with terror. Lightning split the air as bolts of pure white light hit all around her. Thunder crashed throughout the room as the walls shook and the floorboards rattled. Pieces of broken glass were spun into a wrathful fury, each one carrying a reflection of the Siamese cat.

Jenna heard the cries of the animal. They echoed all around her and then gradually faded into the tornado.

A colossal crack of lightning barrelled down through the ceiling as thunder shook the entire house. Jenna screamed in fright, feeling the weight of the world press against her.

And then all was silent. All was still.

MIND TRAP

The room was quiet. No winds. No storm. No Siamese cat. *Is it over? Am I safe?* Jenna was afraid to open her eyes, feeling that the silence was a trap. She'd been fooled before. But there was only one way to know for sure. With what little energy she had left, she forced herself into the moment. Bravely, she opened her eyes.

A life that was once powerful and strong, was no longer there. What stood in its place was something else. With all of her doubts in tow, Jenna searched for familiarity. What she found instead, was change. The ruby was gone. The boxes were gone. The window was gone. The room was gone. Absence was filled with confusion. Answers were replaced with questions.

Her body now stood facing a large empty case. Only air and light occupied the space. The Siamese Mummy had disappeared. And with it went the large wooden coffin, the canopic jars, and the browned, tattered paper. All that existed now was a vacant case, hollow from corner to corner.

Jenna was standing inside the museum.

Looking herself over, she was surprised to see that her injuries had vanished. No broken arm. No swollen head. Only the mental damage lingered. *How did I get here?*

She took a step forward. Lifting one arm, she pressed her hand up against the glass. The frame was cold. She wanted to feel it for herself, to fully understand the capacity of her imagination. "I can't believe that you're really gone. I guess I *did* save you."

She stood for a moment, eyes closed in concentration. With her palm sealed against the glass, she felt a connection to the departed spirit.

"Well, I guess I should thank you, then," a voice appeared behind her.

Jenna's spine nearly rocketed through the roof. In a furious motion, she spun around, clutching what was left of her runaway heart.

Standing by the doorway, was her grandmother.

"Grandma—you're here!" Jenna said, her voice shaking. She could feel the water in her eyes forming.

"Thanks to you, I am," she smiled.

Jenna raced towards her. She nearly knocked her grandmother over as she embraced her. "I thought I lost you!" Tears streamed down her face.

"No, my dear, you could never do that."

Jenna's hold was relentless. She didn't want to let go.

Her grandmother leaned back. "Please, Jenna, I hate to see you cry. I'm here now. Everything's okay."

Reluctantly, she broke her hold. "It was you, wasn't it? You were the soul of the Siamese Mummy."

She nodded and looked at the glass case. "History has been rewritten."

Jenna wiped her eyes with the cuff of her sleeve. She wanted so much to tell someone about her story and prove that it wasn't just a dream. "Who can I tell?"

Her grandmother's response was immediate. "No one must know. Only you and I, for now . . ." Her smile was misleading.

Jenna wondered what that really meant, but still she concurred. "Okay. Just us, for now," she paused. "Wait, what happened to all the animals and the missing—"

"Shh . . ." her grandmother whispered. "Jenna—everyone's fine. The world is as it should be."

With that, Jenna finally began to relax. Everything was back to normal.

Just then, a friendly voice carried down the hallway.

Jenna looked out and saw Anna walking towards them with a clipboard in her hands. "Okay, let's see here . . ."

"Anna!" she cried. "You're here—oh, thank God! I'm so glad you're okay."

"Yes, of course I'm okay. I just went to get the information for the display you were asking about. Why, is something wrong?"

Jenna's grandmother was shaking her head.

"Well . . . um . . . no. Nothing, actually." She gave a flippant smile, then wiped her face with her sleeve. "Don't mind me, I'm just . . ."

Her grandmother stepped in to finish the sentence. "Jenna's just excited to see her brother, Scott. He's coming home today. In fact, we're picking him up at the airport in a few hours."

Jenna did a double take. "We *are*? I mean . . . yes, we are!"

"Oh, that's right," Anna said, her voice chipper. "Your mother told me about that. Well, isn't that exciting. It's too bad that your parents aren't here to greet him, though."

"What do you mean? Where are they?" Jenna's concern came bounding back.

"They're in Spain, dear—remember?" her grandmother grinned.

Jenna's pulse slowly fell back down to Earth. "Oh . . . right . . . of course. I knew that."

"Well, I'm glad we figured that out," Anna said with a smile. She flipped through the papers in her hands. "This display case has been empty for the last week. We're supposed to be receiving some artefacts from King Tutankhamun's tomb, though. They should be arriving on Monday."

"Oh, so it's been empty," Jenna said, exchanging glances with her grandmother.

"Yes, that's right," Anna confirmed. "Well, I better get back to the front desk. You two take care."

"Will do," Jenna said, deep in thought. "Oh, Anna—I wanted to ask you one more thing before you go. How's Sheila's son, Jason?"

"It's funny that you ask. He was just here with his mother talking about you. He said something about a big game tonight at Stamford Park."

"That's right . . . the game. I forgot that was tonight."

"Well, ladies, I must push on. It was lovely to see you both. Abby, always a pleasure."

"Bye, Anna," they said in unison.

Jenna smiled. "Everything is as it should be!" Then, with one final look, she viewed the empty case. The curse of the Siamese Mummy was over. Its reign of terror had ended.

The women locked arms and walked each other out of the room.

"Oh—wait!" Jenna stopped at the escalator. "Grandma—there's just one thing I need to do before we leave. Can you give me ten minutes?"

"Of course. Tell you what, go do what you have to do, and I'll meet you downstairs."

Jenna left her grandmother's side and hurried down the hallway. She walked into another room, passing by several exhibits. When she reached the banner and the giant poster of the Siamese cat, she let out a sigh of relief. "Everything is as it should be."

Now, standing at the foot of the poster, was a concrete podium. And resting on top of it was, *A City Lost,* the black book from Dr. Osiris's house. "He must have stolen this from the museum." But now the book sat in its rightful place. Jenna finally understood why her grandmother had come to visit the room.

She opened the book and thumbed through the pages. It was the story of the Siamese Mummy; she knew it quite well. But there was a new development—the book now had pictures.

In one scene, the Siamese cat was being taken from Menao. Another page showed the Siamese Mummy and the four canopic jars entombed within its case. Jenna's eyes skimmed through the print.

Looking around, she saw no one else in the room. Peering back at the page, she froze. Below, was another picture of the Siamese Mummy, inside the Lionhead Museum. But now, standing in front of the display, was Jenna. With scrutiny, she examined the page.

To prove it was just an anomaly, she skipped ahead until she came to the next picture. This one showed Jenna standing on the street in the rain, being confronted by the Siamese cat. She couldn't believe her eyes. Her fingers rushed through the pages. Jenna appeared throughout the book. "This can't be—how did I become a part of this?"

When her hands rested on the last page, she shuddered. Staring back at her was a picture of the present time, at that very moment. It showed Jenna standing in front of the concrete podium reading the book inside the museum.

She stooped over for a closer inspection of the picture. Hiding in the shadows behind her, was a large animal, waiting. "No—it can't be! This isn't right. This isn't how it's supposed to end!"

As the words escaped her lips, a deep, menacing growl echoed from behind. The colour drained from her face as a deathly shiver crawled up her body. "NO!"

With sheer terror in her eyes, Jenna read the final words on the page.

'For those of you who read this book:
You can only know the truth by being a part of it.
This is not the end, but only the beginning . . .
Beware the Siamese Mummy!'

Photograph by Cheryl Clock

ABOUT THE AUTHOR

 Kara Bartley has always been interested in animals, so it comes as no surprise that her world is surrounded by them in both her life and imagination.

She has a bachelor's degree in Biology/Earth Science, a post-graduate diploma in Geographic Information Systems and a master's degree in Vertebrate Paleontology. In the spring of 2002, she began writing, *The Siamese Mummy,* while on a dig for fossils in Kansas.

Kara is also the author of *The Unearthlings, Call of Adhara and The Moon In Habock's Mirror.* She lives in Niagara Falls, Ontario, with her three Siamese cats Apollo, Achilles and Agamemnon. Her horse, Dapplynn, is her biggest companion and anxiously awaits the day that she too, will have a guest appearance in one of her mother's books.

ABOUT THE ILLUSTRATOR

Tammy Dunlavey grew up in North East, Pennsylvania with the innate ability to draw. When it came to education, Tammy chose science over art, as science offered her a path untaken.

In August of 2001, Tammy was diagnosed with Multiple sclerosis. In light of her medical challenges, she continued on and graduated with a master's degree in Invertebrate Paleontology.

Although Tammy has returned to her artistic roots, she finds that paleontology often appears within her art. Her journey with MS has also played a significant role in her work as her health experiences are well expressed in her creativity.

She is inspired by her son, Keegan, her daughter, Ellen, her granddaughter, Molly-Jane, her husband, Brent and her parents. Tammy's extended family of four-legged pets also provide her with much love and amusement.

THE PALEO TWINS

Tammy and I first met at grad school in the fall of 2002. The first thing I remember her saying to me was, "Oh—*she* must be the Vertebrate Palaeontologist!" From that moment on, we were friends.

We shared an office in the geology department at the University at Buffalo where Tammy studied Invertebrate paleontology and I studied Vertebrate paleontology. Two rival scientists with a common love of fossils and animal history. Who would have known?

Throughout our studies, we talked and travelled. At school we were given the name 'The Paleo Twins' and to our delight, it stuck. Tammy became my sister and for the years we spent in that office, I felt like I had family.

I soon found out that my twin had an amazing flare for artistry, whereas I began to succumb to the creativeness of words. Two scientists turned artists, I'm sure our professors are still scratching their heads.

It was through school that we met as friends but it was paleontology that brought us together as artists.

Our support for one another transcended our education as Tammy and I joined forces once again for this novel. She is the illustrator behind the words and I am the storyteller behind the pictures.

Hopefully this will not be our last creative endeavour.